The Haunted Castle of Oz

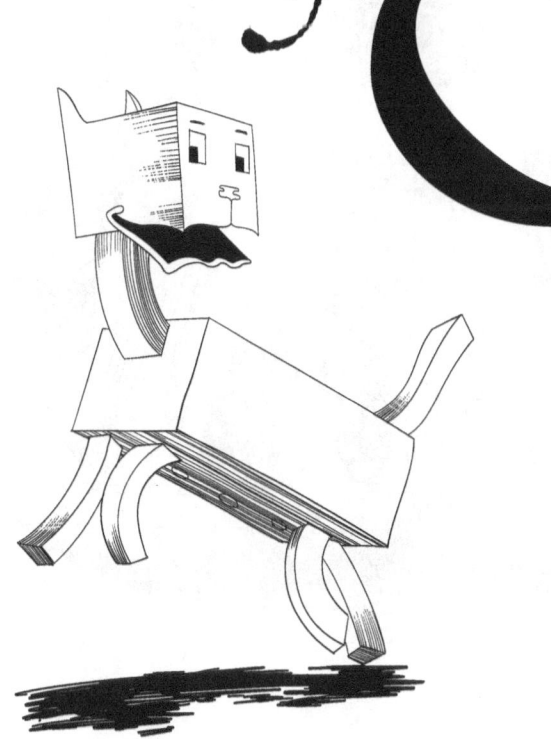

The Haunted Castle of Oz

By Marcus D. Mébès
Illustrated by Kamui Ayami

Founded on and Continuing
the Famous Oz stories by

L. Frank Baum

The Royal Publisher of Oz

May 2019

The Haunted Castle of Oz

10 9 8 7 6 5 4 3 2 1

The Royal Publisher of Oz
Valley Stream, New York

Book design by Marcus D. Mébès
Printed by Lulu publishing: www.lulu.com

Printed in the United States of America
First edition: April 2019

Chapter 1: Ozma's Quandary

IT struck Ozma that the situation she was presented with was quite odd: for a ghost to exist in Oz; in *her* palace of all places... especially since death had been banished in the enchanted land long ago. Aside from a beetle and one of Billina's chicks, Ozma could not easily recall any instances of anyone's demise in her kingdom. From what she knew of ghosts, they were the disembodied spirits of those who had once been alive, but were now not. They haunted the area where they met their demise, but no one had died here in decades. So, why was her castle haunted?

At first only a few palace regulars had noticed him. After all, Ozma's palace, as well as the Emerald City itself was swarming with fantastic people and celebrities, most of whom are so wonderful and magical that a single, diaphanous, quiet man in a suit of armor was dismissed as some delegate or visitor from far off biding his time or enjoying the sights. That is, if he was even seen at all. Jellia

Jamb reported to her queen that at first she thought his appearance was a trick of the light; but, surely, she had indeed seen him. Oscar Diggs, too, had seen the man. Yet, there were times when multiple people would be in his presence, and some see him while others could not.

After having seen this fellow around the palace—in the hallways, cellars, attics, towers, and suites—and nowhere else, certain people became concerned as to who this man was, and his business in being there. True, he carried (in its sheath fortunately) a long-sword, and had in one hand a pointed lance, but the concern was not over any such threat as these might pose. In fact, this person was garbed in a full suit of armor, appearing to be fashioned of gold at times, or even platinum at others. Rather, the concern seemed to be his constant state of melancholy as he wandered about the palace, as if he was in search of something, and disappeared before anyone who glimpsed him could confront him.

"I think he wants to say something," reported Jellia, "but he doesn't make any sound. And just when I look directly at him, he just sort of... pops.

He disappears. It's really quite discouraging." The palace maid clasped her hands in her lap as she spoke with Ozma. She pursed her lips and wrinkled her brow in concern. "I wish we could help him." She looked at the great cats as they slumbered on either side of Ozma, wishing she could be as relaxed as they were.

The queen gently stroked the chicken that was perched next to her, cozily nestled on the arm of her throne. Ozma sighed, nodded, and rose from her throne. "Thank you, Jellia. I will see what we can do. This has gone on long enough. I will not have anyone unhappy in my kingdom. Whoever—or *what*ever—this fellow may be, he has a right to be happy."

The girl ruler requested Jellia to fetch her closest advisors, to meet her in her private suites. Leaving the Cowardly Lion and Hungry Tiger where they napped beside her throne, she quietly strode from the throne room. The only sound to be heard were the click-clacks of her heels as she walked, and the soft clucking of Billina as she, too, napped on Ozma's throne. Turning at the entrance, Ozma looked back, glancing at the green velvet draperies and the crystalline windows. She scrutinized the room, looking in every corner, careful not to miss anything. Seeing nothing, she left.

Yet, as Ozma stepped through the doorway of the throne room into the hallway beyond it, she felt the need to look over her shoulder one last time. Was that a flicker of motion? She observed Billina, the Lion and the Tiger, as well as a potted pothos plant trailing its long tendrils out of the planter. Ozma reminded herself to use the plant's scientific name—*Epipremnum aureum*—as the flying sorcerer Zim had been kind enough to give it to her. Beyond the windows she could see clouds in the sky, a pennant flapping on a turret. But there was nothing else. Bother! This has never happened before!

Ozma made a task of meandering about the castle, slowly nearing her personal suite. It was her intention to scrutinize as much as she could. Searching for the ghost in the Magic Picture had proven fruitless. Whatever made up the fellow was a kind of magic completely foreign to Oz. The Magic Picture would focus on the particular room or hallway that the ghost was in, then try to focus on the ghost itself, flickering back and forth between blur and focus like an automatic camera lens from the great outside world. The vision appearing on the Picture's canvas was enough to give anyone a headache; not that it served to inform her of his whereabouts anyway.

Her efforts to scour the palace were made more laborious due to her cordial nature. Every personage, staff, and guest was glad to see Ozma, and she was obligated to interact with each of them. The girl ruler of Oz was always cordial, always pleasant, and always genuine with each and every one of them. Thus, her trek to her own chamber took much more time than she would have expected, and her attention was not always completely on a ghost hunt.

"That's why I've asked the two of you to help me out," spoke Ozma to the people seated beside her as she reposed at the head of the table in her council chamber.

One was an older gentleman in a silk suit and striped trousers. He wore an old-fashioned tweed vest beneath the silk overcoat. Always dapper, Oscar Diggs was the royal wizard to Her Majesty the Queen Ozma of Oz, and resides in the palace in his own private tower where he can practice and perfect his magical arts. He nodded gravely to his friend and ruler, noting the serious nature of their visit.

The other, a lovely woman garbed in red silks and satins, was the regal Glinda the Good, Sorceress of the South. Glinda wore her hair in a snood, with ringlets falling about to frame her face. She, too, wore a grim expression, and awaited Ozma's appeal.

"I have brought you here to help me solve a mystery that's been plaguing the palace for quite some time now." Ozma pursed her lips and breathed deeply through her nose. A tiny wrinkle of concern creased her forehead, and she looked downward. "It has been one or two weeks now, perhaps."

"You're referring to our infamous 'ghost', I presume," murmured the Wizard as he stirred some sugar into the tea that Jellia Jamb had thoughtfully provided them. Upon her nod, he continued, "I've run into the fellow a few times." He sipped at his tea, grimaced, and dropped two more sugar cubes into it. "Interesting fellow. Seems to me he's looking for something. Ghosts usually have unfinished business to tend to, you know." His head bowed over the tea, he glanced up to meet Ozma's eyes. The Wizard was unable to gauge her reaction, though she remained concerned.

"But if that is the case, then what business has he here?" put in Glinda. "You know as well as I do that ghosts cannot exist in Oz, for there is no death here. Such beings, if that is what they are, would only be extant in the great outside world."

"Ah, but that's where you're wrong, old friend," chided the Wizard. "You'll remember that death seems to have been abolished almost a hundred years ago; say, around the

beginning of Ozma's reign as queen of this marvelous land."
He sipped at the tea, swallowed, and continued. "And
regardless of whether or not he's a ghost, and regardless of
whether or not he's from here, he *can* exist. We've all seen
him. Perhaps he's come from elsewhere."

"Whatever the case may be," interrupted Ozma, "I'd
like to know how we can deal with this ghost, if ghost he
really is... or even if we *should* deal with him." She looked
askance at the Wizard. "If he's from elsewhere, is his status
as a ghost something we need to concern ourselves with?
Rather, I'd like to find out what's bothering the poor fellow,
and see if we can help him out!"

"If I gather aright, Ozma," said Glinda, "then you are
asking us whether to interfere with this being's business
by assisting him in his search, in order to eliminate the
mystery of his being here."

"Pretty much. I am asking just that. However, according
to our friends from the great outside world, ghosts are
pretty tricky, and in fact, Notta assures me that's just what
this ghost is: tricky. Oscar, you're from America originally.
Surely you must know how to deal with a ghost."

"Ah... Notta Bit More and Bob Up. Those two might
know about ghosts." The Wizard made a mental note to
track down the clown and the boy at their circus. "To
tell the truth, ghosts aren't as common as you might
think. However," he added quickly, detecting a hint of
disappointment on the fairy's face, "I had a gypsy friend...
back in my carnival days. I believe her name was Griselda
or Hilda or something. Whatever name she felt like
using, depending on where we traveled." He smiled at the
reminiscence. "Anyway, she claimed to have dealt with
ghosts before. She conducted séances to speak with these

dear departed folks, find out what their problem was, get about correcting it, and if she couldn't, well then she'd get Father Patrick O'Brien away from his bottle of whiskey to bless those poor souls and send 'em on their way." He set his cup of tea down on the table and regarded it. Remembering another man's vice with the drink rankled his composure. "Poor fella."

"Religion is not that prominent in Oz," reminded Glinda after she finished her cup of tea. "I will *not* perform a séance, nor do I know what the people's reactions to it would be. Such black magic is forbidden. Nor do I know how to bless a soul and send it on its way."

The conversation seemed to disturb the sorceress, and the girl ruler was concerned with Glinda's reaction. "I'm afraid we're going to have to figure out another way to deal with our guest," sighed Ozma. "It *is* agreed that something must be done, right?"

The other two nodded, then fell silent. What must be done? Never before in Oz history did such a quandary present itself. After much deliberation, in the end it was decided that those who had the most experience, if any at all, in great outside world, should be consulted.

The Gale family—Dorothy, Aunt Em, and Uncle Henry—as well as Trot Griffiths, Betsy Bobbin, and Button Bright were invited to confer with the three. Cap'n Bill Wheedles was preparing to head off to the Nonestic on some official business with the Sea Fairies and Captain Salt, but Ozma intercepted his departure. The Shaggy Man seemed to have no interest at all in the endeavor, nor did his brother. All seven of those gathered were familiar with the concept of ghosts; however, none had any experience to tell of, at least not openly. Both Em and Henry seemed quite agitated once they were informed that they were dealing with the supernatural.

"I reckon I don't wish to have anything to do with no ghost," demurred Em nervously as she held her hand to her heart. Henry, standing behind her, put his hand on her shoulder protectively and wholeheartedly agreed with her sentiment. Despite having lived for many decades in the magical land of Oz where scarecrows and rag dolls

danced and animals talked, somehow the concept of the supernatural was unsettling to the old farm couple.

Dorothy, on the other hand, although sympathizing with her beloved aunt and uncle, was more willing to be involved, as were Trot, Button Bright, and Betsy. The children volunteered readily. "This sounds like it could be really int'resting!" she spoke up, smiling eagerly to bolster the mood in the room. "I'd love to help out. How... well, what can we do?"

"Okay," murmured Button Bright, smiling. Since the boy had come to terms with his Yookoohoo heritage, he had an air of confidence about him that gave him peace in nearly any situation.

"I'll help, too!" offered Betsy Bobbin and Tiny Trot together. They giggled, dropping their faces to smile at each other. "Ghosts!" whispered Trot to Betsy. "Isn't it wonderful?"

Behind Trot, Cap'n Bill coughed and shook his head. "Just here ta consult, yer majesty. Ye know I've got business with Salt and Aquareine. Somethin' about an egg." He coughed again, and went silent.

Oscar Diggs looked to Ozma for permission, then answered Dorothy's question. "Well, we'd like to track down this ghost, and see if we can communicate with him."

"Apparently," added Glinda, "this has not yet been done because of various reasons. Either he disappears before anyone can try to speak with him, or people's attentions are distracted and he disappears. Whatever the case is, the end result is that he always disappears."

"Which," added the Wizard, "is why I'm giving you my search-light." He reached into the black bag at his feet and removed an item that resembled a pen-sized flashlight.

"I've got a button on it, right here," he said, tapping at its side, "that'll freeze whatever you catch in the light."

"Seems well 'n good ta me," observed Cap'n Bill, "but won't a light shine right through a ghost?"

"Oh... erh... ahem..." The Wizard was at a loss for words. "I hadn't considered that, but..."

"Let's try anyway," offered Dorothy, reaching for the searchlight. She accepted it, and tucked it into a pocket of her dress. "Thanks."

"I don't really know if I can offer you anything magical," spoke Ozma to her friends, "seeing as how we've never had to deal with a ghost before, and I could not even begin to guess what you could or couldn't use."

"However," added Glinda, "you will be given a safety precaution to protect you should anything... unforeseen occur." Glinda arose and walked around the table, placing a kiss on all four children's foreheads. "Ozma, the Wizard, and I will take turns watching the four of you in the Magic Picture. Unfortunately, our duties require our attention a great deal of the time, or we'd personally accompany you."

"Mind you don't do anything foolish," warned the Wizard. "Who knows what that ghost might do, or what might happen to him."

"I'm sure we'll be able to handle this just fine, Wiz," replied Dorothy honestly. "Do you have any ideas for what we might do?"

"Actually," hedged the Wizard, blushing a bit, "we thought we'd leave that up to you. You see, er... ahem..."

"What Oscar is trying to say, dears," spoke Glinda patiently, "is that we'd like to rely on your own judgment and ideas. Each of you seem to have qualities that would help, such as Dorothy's ingenuity or Trot's ability to get out of a jam."

"It seems okay to me," mused Button Bright as he leaned back on the hind legs of his chair.

"Me too," added Betsy a bit more excitedly. "This'll be fun! I've never met a ghost before!"

"*Meeting* him will be the first obstacle," noted Ozma cryptically.

Chapter 2: On Redecorating Unused Palace Wings

"**O**ZMA sure wasn't kidding," sighed Dorothy as she and her three friends wandered about the palace. "We haven't seen hide nor hair of this ghost." She ran her fingers along the intricate designs carved into a green marble pillar, absent-mindedly letting her mind wander.

"No kidding!" added Trot. "We've been wandering around the castle for hours now! I didn't know some of these rooms even existed!" The black-haired little girl twisted the knob of a door, opened it to reveal a broom closet, and looked around inside it before shutting it again. "It's dusty! Just how big is Ozma's palace anyway?"

"Heck!" put in Betsy. "I'd forgotten this entire wing of the palace existed! Why, we're four levels up off the ground, and we haven't even covered *half* the place yet!"

A sudden whirl of color jolted them to attention as two figures rounded a corner hallway and appeared before them. Both were covered from head to toe in a spectrum of colors. One was a lovely cloud fairy and the other was a girl made out of a patchwork quilt.

"Polly! Scraps!" The children were instantly covered with kisses and squeezed in hugs.

"Oh my goodness!" sighed Dorothy. "It's so good to see you!"

"It is nice to see you both," commented Button Bright after disentangling himself from Scraps' arms. "But this isn't working and the constant distractions are tiresome." At a hurt look from Scraps, he amended. "Not you." He hugged her back, once again tangling himself up in her rag-doll arms. "It's this search. Maybe we should just try to bring him to us... instead of us trying to find him." He wondered if his Yookoohoo magic could transform him into something that could track spirits.

"What brings you all here?" asked the Rainbow's daughter of the group of children. "This is a part of the palace people rarely visit." She swept her arms up over her head and pirouetted around merrily. "Scraps and I are trying to decide how to redecorate it and make it more attractive, so more people would come up here!"

"Makes no sense to have such a huge palace and the rooms unoccupied," added Scraps, sticking out her tongue. She patted Button Bright on the head. "What's your story?"

"We're ghost hunting," piped up Trot emphatically.

"You don't say!" breathed Polychrome, kneeling down to look her friends in the eyes. "The knight? The handsome fellow in the suit of armor? Oh, he's so sad!" She clasped her hands to her heart and sighed. "And *so* handsome. Did I mention that?"

Scraps smiled at Button Bright, who rolled his eyes, then patted his back as he walked away from the group.

The Patchwork Girl then slapped her gloved hand on the back of Polychrome's head, upsetting her cap and nearly toppling the Rainbow's daughter. "Feh. He's sad all right. Don't get her started on how h-a-n-d-s-o-m-e she thinks he is."

Polychrome stood up and dusted off her dress. "There's nothing wrong with stating the obvious." She crossed her arms over her chest and huffed.

"Then why state it?" asked Scraps. "It's obvious to *you*. But talking about it over, and over, and over, and over again can get... what'd Button Bright say? Tiresome."

Polychrome said nothing. She stared upward and ignored her colorful friend.

Trot spoke up before Scraps could further antagonize their friend. "Dorothy and Betsy and Button..." She turned about in a circle, looking up and down the hallway they were in. "Say, where's Button Bright?"

"He was just here," answered Betsy.

"He left!" stated Scraps, turning a backward somersault. "Bet he thinks this conversation's tiresome."

"I'll bet you anything he went back to that reading room down the hallway. You know, right after Eureka told us that she saw something moving in there," replied Dorothy.

"I thought it was the Woozy who said that," said Betsy.

"No, that was on the second floor, after we ran into the Shaggy Man," replied Dorothy, scratching her chin.

"It's been minutes," said Polychrome. "He's on this floor. He walked that way, right? Let's just go back the direction you came from and find him."

"But he could be *any*where," fussed Dorothy, slumping her shoulders.

"Then let's get going," said Scraps impatiently. "Let's just all go back there and get him." She sauntered down the hallway, looking behind her to ensure the others were following. Turning a cartwheel as she arrived at the reading room door, she allowed the others to catch up before turning the doorknob. With a smile, she noticed that Button Bright's skeleton key was in the lock, and that the door was already ajar. "After you," she spoke in *sotto voce* as she opened it, allowing the others to enter.

Sure enough, slumped on an oversized leather easy chair was Button Bright, sleeping peacefully.

"That was fast," commented Trot quietly. She looked at the others, sharing their bemusement at how swiftly the boy could fall asleep. "No matter how old or how much experience he has, he'll always be Button Bright." She smiled and rolled her eyes.

"It *is* late," suggested Dorothy. "How long have we been searching?" She looked at her friends, and added, "What time is it?"

"Guessing it's about midnight or thereabouts," whispered Scraps, gingerly tiptoeing around the room and peering around pieces of furniture. "No ghosts in here!"

"Midnight? Ugh," groused Betsy. "No wonder I'm so tired."

"Definitely past bed-time," agreed Trot, yawning greatly into her hand. She looked at her companions, seeing that only Scraps and Polychrome were alert and vibrant. "I guess he's got the right idea. I *am* tired."

"Oh, but ghosts are more active at night!" insisted Dorothy. "We can't give up the search yet!" She stepped into the hallway and peered anxiously in both directions.

"I'm not suggesting that," responded Trot quickly. "Maybe if we just take a quick nap... Scraps and Polly could wake us up if they see anything."

"Sure," agreed the Patchwork Girl as she carefully pushed a chair from the corner of the room closer to the center where she had gathered two others besides the one occupied by the sleeping boy. She managed to pull them together without making any noise to wake up Button Bright. "We're going to be up here for a while anyway."

"All right, I guess," acquiesced Dorothy, shrugging her shoulders. She slumped toward one of the chairs. "A little nap," she yawned, "couldn't hurt. Thirty minutes."

"Of course!" ushered Scraps and pushing her toward the chair. "You meat people have to get your rest. We'll be right here."

Polychrome smiled and nodded.

Dorothy, Trot and Betsy no sooner had made themselves cozy in the big easy chairs before they nodded off. Polychrome and Scraps waited until they could hear the children's steady breathing before they shuffled to the door of the room.

"Well, Poly dear," whispered Scraps, "we've already looked this room over. Let's go down the hall a bit." She threw her hands up and waved around the room. "This room is *boooring*! It needs more color and light!"

"Shhh!" urged Polychrome as Scraps' voice grew louder. She covered the Patchwork Girl's mouth with her delicate hand. "All right," agreed the Rainbow's daughter. "But we have to be back in half an hour to wake them up."

"Of course," chuckled her friend as she opened the door and tip-toed out. "Come on!"

"Just a minute," called Polychrome in a hushed whisper. She strode gingerly to the mantle where a solitary lamp lit up the entire room. Turning the knob slowly at its base, she lowered the wick into the kerosene, dimming the room sufficiently so as not to wake up the slumbering occupants.

Closing the door with a soft click behind them, Polychrome and Scraps failed to notice that the key that Button Bright had used to unlock the door was still sticking in the keyhole—on the outside of the door.

"A definite chartreuse," observed Polychrome, staring intently at an old and faded set of velvet curtains adorning a pair of balcony windows. She gazed dreamily into the night sky beyond.

"Are you nuts?" shrieked Scraps. "Purple with green spots! Or maybe pink with olive checks!"

"In your dreams! Those colors clash!" Polychrome dragged the absurd girl further down the hallway. "This carpeting has *got* to go! We need a bright emerald green, not this dark pine green."

"Mauve," drawled Scraps as if lost in thought. "Mauve with gold diamonds."

Their voices trailed down the hallway and around a corner where they eventually faded as the two maidens of color were incurably caught up in their discussion.

In the silent hallway, a shimmering figure laid its hand upon the door knob and turned. Finding it locked, it did not bother to turn the key, but instead passed through the door as if it was only an intangible illusion.

Chapter 3
Something Stirring in the Room

BUTTON BRIGHT stirred in his chair. Something had interrupted his sleep... something cold. As he turned himself about and sat upright in the chair he noticed that the room that had been warm and inviting not more than an hour ago was now quite cold and dark. And not only that, but his three friends were curled up and shivering on three other chairs next to his.

Silently looking around, Button Bright saw nothing out of the ordinary, but he still felt a chill of discomfort emanating from some place nearby. His innate magical senses were firing, telling him that there was something else with them in the room.

Without a sound he slid off the chair and carefully nudged his sleeping companions awake.

"Brrr!" shivered Trot, hugging herself as she stared about the room with widened eyes. "I didn't realize how *big* this room was... or how c-cold!"

"But this isn't possible," whispered Dorothy nervously

as she, too, took in the room anew. "The palace is always kept at a comfortable temperature. Every room! Besides, the weather outside is always near perfect anyway."

"Something eerie is going on here," muttered Betsy gloomily. "I want to go back to my own room!" She rose off the chair and headed for the door. Turning the handle to no avail, she turned back to the others in fear. "It's locked! Where's the key?"

Trot fumbled in the pouch pocket of her skirt. "It's not here. I thought I gave it to..." She looked at the boy.

Button Bright sheepishly looked downward.

"Don't worry," assured Dorothy. "Remember? Someone's always watching us in the Magic Picture. We don't want to give up just yet though. It's not right. Besides... What if the ghost is here?" Dorothy's voice was a hushed whisper as she spoke her last question, the excitement brilliant in her eyes.

A hushed tension befell the room. All four huddled with their backs together, facing outward, scanning the room.

"I-If there's anyone here," faltered Dorothy after some hesitation, "Why don't you come on out? We just want to t-talk to you..." She fumbled her hand into the pocket of her dress, grasping the Wizard's searchlight.

The silence was unnerving as they waited for a reply.

After nearly five minutes of anxious suspense, a soft, male voice drifted out to them. "Are... are there just the four of you?" he asked, in a cracking voice.

"Yes!" answered Dorothy quickly, heartened at the gentleness of the voice. "It's just me, Dorothy, and Trot, and Betsy, and Button Bright here." She curtsied in the general area from where the voice had emanated. "I'm a

Princess of Oz, and..."

"A *Princess*?" cried the voice suddenly. Instantly, a handsome young man dressed in knight's garb emerged from the shadows and knelt before Dorothy. "My prayers have been answered! My search ends! I have found my salvation!" He grasped her hand in his and planted a kiss upon her palm.

Dorothy had only enough time to reach backward and grasp Trot's outstretched hand as the knight, Dorothy, Trot, Button Bright, and Betsy vanished in a brilliant flash of light.

"Dadgum it!" blurted out the Wizard of Oz as he was caught nodding off in front of the Magic Picture. "Jellia! Jellia Jamb!" he yelled, pulling a bell-cord to summon the maid. "Get Ozma and Glinda now!" He stood quite agitated before the Magic Picture, commanding it, "Show me Dorothy and Trot and Betsy and Button Bright right now!"

The screen shifted to one of the several generic pictures that appeared on the screen whenever the Picture was not in use: a dreary, yet still majestic castle set upon a high crag of rocks, surrounded by storm clouds in the night sky.

In mere moments, Glinda and Ozma found an exasperated Oscar Diggs pacing in front of the Picture muttering repeatedly, "I've lost them." He looked up upon their entrance and repeated, "I've lost them!"

With frightened eyes, Ozma looked imploringly at Glinda, whose only response was a worrisome countenance. "They do have my magical blessing with them," she added encouragingly as they joined the Wizard to sit on the couch, staring at the generic view of a medieval castle.

"What are we looking at?" asked the sorceress of the south. She regarded the image of the castle amid the crags of a mountain top. It was an image she had seen before, but never truly paid mind to. This image—and many other nondescript pictures—passed across the Magic Picture's canvas at random when the device was simply decorative.

"I don't understand it," sighed Oscar Diggs dejectedly. "I command it to show me the children, and all it shows me is this, and I've seen this picture enough times to know that this place does not exist!"

"What do you mean, 'not exist?' The Magic picture shows everything in Oz we want to see. Even in the great outside world." Glinda crossed her arms and glared at the picture.

"That's exactly what I mean," the Wizard replied anxiously. "They're not *in* Oz. Not in Nonestica. They're not even in the great outside world. I have *no* earthly idea where they've gone!"

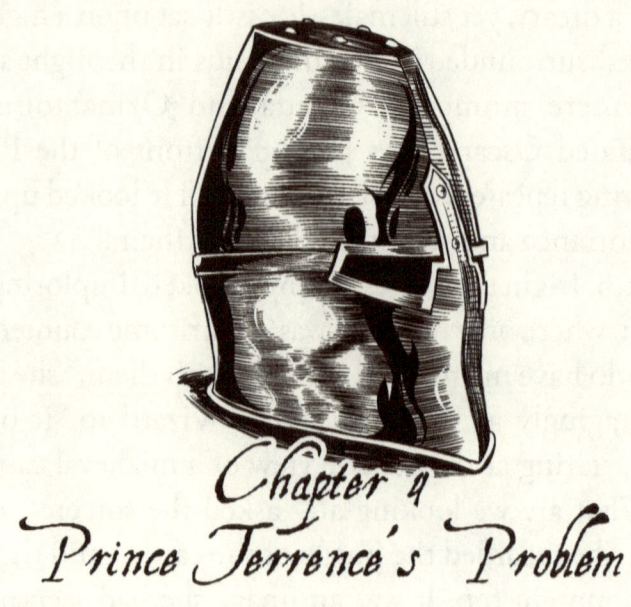

Chapter 9
Prince Terrence's Problem

DOROTHY, Trot, Button Bright, and Betsy found themselves, along with the knight, in a leaky stone tower room. Through a small open window, they could see that the tower was situated beside an otherwise majestic castle that looked as if it was just about to go into ruin. Standing before the bewildered quartet was a wizened old gentleman in long, billowing robes. Blinding, brilliant light filled the room, but they could make out his appearance. From his chin the white whiskers pointed an arrow to the stone floor, and his head was covered with a cowl.

Bursts of energy emanated from the old man's outstretched hands, and as he lowered them to his sides, the light faded and their eyes recovered from the momentary blindness.

The older man strode to the young man's side. "Didst thou succeed in thy quest?" inquired the elder of the

knight. "Who be these children?"

"Verily, I did succeed, Master Necronimus." The knight waved his arms in a flourish, presenting Dorothy and her companions. "She is a princess." He patted her head. "And she is solid. All of them are!"

"Perhaps later, then, thou wilt explain to me why thou acquired three other children along with thy bride-to-be."

Dorothy's face paled as she and her companions were rendered dumbstruck. She could not speak, but merely uttered incoherently.

"Come now, Master Terrence," the elder directed as he bustled the small crowd toward a trap-door in the tower room. Above it, on the wall, was a small window through which Dorothy and the others were able to glimpse the castle, enshrouded as it was with voluminous storm clouds. "We mustn't allow anyone to see thou here, lest thy uncle deduce our scheme."

"Come! We must hurry. Please." The knight, Terrence, extended a hand imploringly to Dorothy. He led the speechless children down a spiral staircase in the tower, and then out in the open along the castle turrets to cross down another, precarious stairway that was dangerously exposed to the harsh outer elements. Seeing that they had no alternatives, they meekly followed the young man as he dashed down the steps and into an anteroom within the large castle.

Once inside, Terrence leapt to the door that led out into the rest of the castle and rattled the bolt on it, assuring himself that they were securely locked in the ante-room. He then ran past the children and closed the swinging doors that led to the tower.

Finally, assured that they were alone and protected from intrusion, the knight fell once again on his knees before Dorothy. "At long last," he sighed to her, breathless from his exertion. Holding her hand in his own, he looked imploringly into her eyes. "You are but a child, I know, but in time you shall mature. I am patient to wait in return of the great favor you shall do me. With thy leave, we shall be wed on the morrow, and all my troubles shall vanish!" He closed his eyes in tremendous relief... only to have it taken away as Dorothy fearfully withdrew her hand.

"I'm not marrying you!" she exclaimed vehemently. "I don't *know* you! And even if I did..."

Taken aback, Terrence rose, and pleaded with her, panicked, "I apologize, your majesty. Please do accept my sincerest apologies. But thou must! There is no other alternative." He looked desperately at Button Bright, Betsy, and Trot. "Please, do hear me. Yes, you are but a child, yet thou art my only hope in this dismal time. I implore you. I beseech you. Please help me!"

"We're not doing *any*thing 'til you answer Dorothy's questions," stated Trot sternly, as she folded her arms across her chest and stood her ground.

"Yeah," added Button Bright. "It appears to me that you need something from us, and we're not going to give you anything until you tell us your business."

Looking at all four stern—and alarmed—faces, the young man quickly composed himself and rose. "Please pardon my lack of composure and accept my apology," he stated, making a deep, stately bow. "Allow me to introduce myself. My name is Squire... er, I mean to say *Sir* Terrence, Knight of the Lance, Prince of the Kingdom of Flora—in which you are—in my father King Flora's castle, currently ruled by my uncle Prince Regent Gorsbenor."

"Okay," replied Dorothy courteously. "I'm Dorothy, she's Trot, she's Betsy, and he's Button Bright."

"*Princess* Dorothy?" put in Terrence hopefully.

"Yes," she replied, "of Oz. Trot and Betsy are princesses, too."

"I only need to marry *one* princess to become eligible for kingship," informed the knight, smiling sadly. The desperation in his eyes was clouded over by the disappointment that the only princess he could locate appeared to be half his own age.

"Just what is this all about?" asked Dorothy. "I'm too young to marry, even if I wanted to, which I don't. How old are you anyway?"

"I am eighteen years of age, Princess," he replied, "but age does not matter. You are... fourteen? That is more than half my age. We are not so many years apart. "

"So he thinks," whispered Button Bright sarcastically into Trot's ear, calling to mind the Ozians' ability to stop aging. "We must be in a magical land," he added.

"I know," replied the little girl, "else we'd have grown up." She shuddered, recalling the time when they were transported to the outside world and began to age. If any of them were to mature into their proper ages... well, that would be very unfortunate. "Where is Flora anyway? Is it beyond the Deadly Desert?"

"Deadly Desert?" echoed the knight. "I'm afraid I do

not follow." He addressed the others. "My mad uncle Gorsbenor," Sir Terrence continued, "promised me that he would only sit upon the throne until I find a princess to be my queen. Our laws dictate that the heir to the throne must be wed to one of noble birth before he may claim it. 'Tis only for the people of course. Uncle tells me our people need a queen. But I believe that he wants to be king of Flora himself. He has been keeping me under constant watch whenever I am not being secluded in the castle. But I had a special key he knew not of!"

The older man, Necronimus, deigned to make himself known, startling the children who had forgotten about his being there with them.

"I worked an enchantment that would send Terrence, in an insubstantial state of being, to a castle that my magicks informed me was abounding with princesses. 'Twas our hope that there he could find one to marry. Gorsbenor had not counted on our resourcefulness." He folded his arms in the sleeves of his robes and grinned. "Foolish law though it may be, we will abide by it. 'Tis only proper to set a good example." He turned to Trot. "You asked where Flora is. I'm afraid you will not find it in your dimension." He glowered mysteriously, making the little girl shudder.

"Wait a minute," cut in Dorothy. Though she truly appeared to be a child, Dorothy Gale was by far older than the prince, and had gained a great deal of wisdom in her long life. "You yourself called your uncle mad, and you believe he wants the kingdom for himself. What makes you think your *mad* uncle is going to let you be king just because you presume to have found your bride? *Assuming* I'll marry you, which I seriously doubt, what proof do you have that your uncle will keep his word?"

"Nuh-uh! Not us!" denied both Trot and Betsy together as Terrence's glance turned hopefully to them.

"'Tis a chance I must take," replied Terrence, his attention once more on Dorothy. He looked thoughtful for a moment. "As... as reprehensible as the situation is, I must abide by the law." He furrowed his brow in worry, glancing at the wizard for guidance. "Perhaps... perhaps we can make a deal. We could declare our betrothal, uncle will abdicate the throne to me, I will then banish him, and Necronimus can then return thee to thy home?"

"Thou art young, truly," sighed Necronimus, reaching out to touch the knight's head. He brushed his fingers through Terrence's hair and smiled sadly at him. "You still are innocent in many ways." He looked at the children. "I ask thee, though children you may *appear* to be, to confer with me... as adults. You are indeed older than you appear to be, are you not?"

Dorothy, Trot, Betsy and Button Bright exchanged glances. An eyebrow raised, lips clenched, and darted eyes all communicated to the wizard that his assessment was accurate. He could tell that the world they came from was quite unlike Flora.

Dorothy wrinkled her brow in thought. "I... *we* need to think this over." She turned back to her friends, ushering them far enough away from the wizard and the knight to confer privately. "What should I do?" she asked of them. "He seems honest enough. Poor guy! I wonder if he really believes he has a chance."

"I don't like that uncle of his already!" whispered Button Bright. "I bet he won't let him be king even *if* he marries you."

Dorothy regarded each of her friends in turn. "What

do you think?" she asked Trot, who happened to be the youngest of the group.

"I think we oughtta help him," she answered honestly. "He really needs our help! Look at him." Four pairs of eyes regarded the despairing prince.

"Just wait a minute, now," suggested Betsy. "I would like to know one thing." She strode back to Terrence and Necronimus and demanded, "Just exactly *why* is it so important for you to be king anyway? Why are you so sad that he's king and you're not? What makes you a better king? And what will you do *if* you become king?"

"Good questions!" muttered Button Bright, nodding slowly.

"Well... indeed... I..." Terrence looked at his inquisitor and her companions. "I suppose I should be a good king, and rule the land justly and wisely."

"Can you be sure?" asked Trot. She glanced at the wizard, who closed his eyes and nodded. "Will Necronimus be an advisor? Do you have anyone you can trust? How big is your kingdom?"

Terrence fumbled with the questions, attempting to answer them all. "Of course Necronimus will give me counsel. There are few I can trust, but still, my page..." He paused. The wizard, keen to the prince's habits, had already pulled a chair forward and offered it to the knight. Sitting, Terrence rested his arms on his legs and leaned downward. "The kingdom of Flora is small. It is... mountainous. The people have departed the kingdom for the most part. My uncle... he speaks of raising an army... but the people are gone. We have been called an inhospitable terrain..."

"With inhospitable clime as well," added the Wizard. He placed his hand upon Terrence's shoulder. "It appears

that these *children* have succeeded in an endeavor that I have not." He winked and grinned mysteriously at them. "Pray, go on. Have you more questions?"

"Why is it so important for you to be king?" asked Dorothy, returning to address the prince.

Swallowing, Terrence looked up and met her gaze. His eyes were moist, and his lips trembled. He pulled the armored gloves off his hands and tossed them to the floor. Wiping his hands over his face and then back over his head, he sighed. "Because it is all that I have left," he answered sadly. He punctuated his next words with a pause between each one. "It has all been taken from me. *Everything.*"

Dorothy felt his pain and loss, and took his hand in hers. "Tell me."

The other children gathered around the seated knight. Button Bright sat down cross-legged on the floor, but Betsy and Trot stood with Dorothy.

The wizard waved his hands in the air and conjured chairs for each of them. "Do sit, honored guests. What little comforts we have, we shall share with you."

Terrence inhaled deeply through his nose, and let the breath out in one long sigh. "My uncle took everything from me. He will continue to take, and take, and take, until there is nothing left to take. I will stop him. I *must* stop him." He shrugged. "And how can he build an army with only the few guards that remain?"

"A vendetta? Revenge?" asked Betsy quietly, but Dorothy shushed her friend before Terrence could reply.

"He even took my hound," whimpered Terrence, once again dropping his head downward. "Angus."

The prince of Flora related to the gathered Ozians his tale of woe. "'Twas not but a year ago. Less, perhaps." He sighed, and looked at the wizard. "Mireille."

The older man sucked in a breath and spat out the name. "Mireille. Bah! The wench was your uncle's servant. Not thine. Her intentions were ill from the beginning." Though the others sat, Necronimus remained standing, a shadowy figure behind the prince.

"I have a dog, too," Dorothy said softly. "His name's Toto."

Terrence sniffled. "Aye. The funny little black dog. He has been very friendly to me."

"What? Oh! Toto!" Dorothy felt like scolding her pet,

had he been there with her. "You've seen him?"

"Verily I have, your majesty. He and the other animals living in your palace have been the few to communicate with me."

"But we've *tried*," insisted Betsy Bobbin, tilting her head. "Why has it been so hard to talk with you?"

"My powers," explained the Wizard, "vast though they may be, are nothing compared to the magicians of thy world. I did my best to send Terrence to thy abode, to beseech of thee aid. 'Tis a spell that wearies me, and as such, Terrence appeared to thee only as a spirit."

"At nighttime, when there were only few awake for me to encounter, was when Necronimus' power was at its best."

"I am strongest when there are fewer about to take my energy; be it in this world or thine." The wizard shrugged, letting the cowl fall over his eyes.

"And at such times I encountered your pet."

Dorothy nodded, still holding Terrence's hand. "What about your dog?"

Terrence's eyes narrowed. "Mireille killed him."

The children gasped as one.

Button Bright was the first to speak. "What happened?" he asked sadly.

Slumped in the chair, Terrence stared off into the darkness of the room. "Uncle sent her to entice me. To distract me. She was good at her duties, and performed them well. My father had not yet been cold a month when Uncle sent her to me. In my despair, I succumbed to her touch." He looked up. "I was lonely."

Necronimus spat in derision, wrinkling his nose in distaste.

"My hound—Angus was his name—would have none of the wench. He despised her from the start." Terrence smiled, in spite of himself, "He bit at her heels and tore her dress. She wanted me to send him away, but I did not. My Angus... my Angus was loyal. To the end." Terrence closed his eyes. "Mireille stole his life from him one night after our dalliances. I was asleep, and she... ran him through with... with a dagger."

"The animal's howls were enough to wake the castle," informed the wizard, his lips curled back in a distasteful sneer. "It was my duty to heal, and those I could not heal, I hasten from their pain. Angus' pain was short lived." He tightened his grip on Terrence's shoulder, then relaxed it again. After a pause, he added, "And then I shortened Mireille's pain as well."

The children didn't need to ask Necronimus what he meant by that statement.

Chapter 5: The Loyal Friendship of a Page

AFTER some quick deliberation, Dorothy stepped forward and confronted Terrence. "Well, Terrence," she began, "you suggested that we announce a betrothal. Your suggestion seems to be the best option, assuming it'll work. I guess I'm willing to go through with this act to help you out. I don't know how your people will feel about you springing a bride upon them out of nowhere, but... well, we've encountered things that are *a lot* more hard to believe. Besides, it looks like this has already turned into an adventure for us."

"Praise be to Elion," he exclaimed. "I promise thee, Princess, that we will only go through with the charade until I am king. Then thou art free to go home. I cannot begin to tell thee how grateful I am!"

"Just... just how long do you expect this process to be?" asked Dorothy. Having lived the life of royalty as long as she had, the princess knew full well that ceremonies— especially *royal* ceremonies—had the tendency to drag on and on for extended periods of time. "It's not that we're in a hurry," she explained, "but we have people back home who are likely worried about us."

"Her point is valid, Terrence," commented the wizard. "Just how long *do* we expect this charade to last?"

"I... I don't really know," replied the flustered prince. "This is all so unfamiliar to me." He imploringly gazed at the people around him. "Why can't my life be like it was before? I had no responsibilities. It was so *easy*."

"Well, that was *before*," stated Betsy, interrupting his misery. "For starters, you can get us out of this cooped up room. I for one could use something to eat, also."

"Me too," put in Button Bright, nodding his head emphatically. "I'm starved!" In frustration, he had tried to use his Yookoohoo powers, and found the ability had failed him. He chose not to mention that to his friends.

Given a clear task, Terrence was glad to be able to focus. "Of course, of course," he agreed readily. "But we must be discrete. I fear my uncle could be quite vexed should he discover your presence." He arose and proceeded to unbolt the door. "Do follow me. I will have one of my *loyal* servants see to your needs."

"You have *disloyal* servants?" asked Trot, believing that a servant had to be loyal in order to be a servant, and could not understand why one would keep a *dis*loyal one.

He nodded as he opened the door. "Necronimus is not a servant, but he is loyal to me. He is my friend."

"And I have business to attend to," added the old wizard, nodding his head curtly. He took an appraising look of the children through narrowed eyes, and smiled. "I shall take my leave for the moment. We shall be reunited soon. Never fear." With that, he swept out of the opened door and disappeared among the dark shadows.

The four Ozians were led down a dimly lit corridor that had tapestries of all sorts, paintings, suits of armor, and marble busts dotting the hallway at various intervals. The tapestries depicted happy people tending sheep and goats on hillsides, raising crops on plateaus, attending festivals, and dancing. The colors were bright, but all were covered with thick layers of dust and grime, indicating that the castle had not been well upkept in quite some time.

"Are those your parents?" asked Button Bright, pointing to a magnificently large painting that hung in an ornate frame above the entry to a balcony. A thin man in fine regalia posed next to a plump woman with a genial smile. Both had merry twinkles in their eyes, and pleasant expressions. "You look like them," the boy added after scrutinizing the painting.

Turning a corner, they were confronted by a large oaken door. "This is my private chamber," Terrence informed them, opening the door and entering. Once the others were securely inside, Terrence bolted the door behind them and pulled a cord hanging from the ceiling beside the entry.

"It's very nice," murmured Betsy, looking about at the room. It was small, with stone walls, a small fireplace, a bed, table, chairs, and a bookshelf. Small windows opened out to reveal the desolate, mountainous terrain of Flora. She could not help but wonder why on earth the kingdom was so inappropriately named.

Trot stepped in front of the bookshelf and began reading the titles along one row when Terrence stood next to her. "Please, we should step back," he admonished, ushering her away from it.

Before too long a boy emerged from behind the

bookshelf. It swung open on hinges, revealing a rough-hewn passageway behind it. He carried with him a covered platter which he set upon a writing table. Lifting the lid revealed a carafe of red wine, a loaf of bread, and a large slice of cheese.

"Will there be anything else, sir, before I leave thee?" asked the boy of his liege. He gazed wide-eyed at the three girls and boy with Terrence, and gulped. "I do not believe I brought enough food," he stammered.

"No, no, Christian," replied Terrence, gratefully smiling at the boy. "But... *do* stay. 'Tis been quite some time since I've seen a friendly face. They are few and far between in these dark days." Terrence grinned and opened his arms outward.

"Of course," said the boy, who proceeded to unlace the plates of metal of Terrence's armor. "I will have this off thee in a moment."

"No!" Terrence threw off an arm plate with a clatter and hugged the boy close to him. Christian, nervous to show affection for his friend in front of the strangers, stiffened, then melted to hug him back.

Pushing himself from Terrence's embrace, the boy continued to help the knight remove the rest of the armor. "I may be the last soul friendly to you in this entire castle... other than Necronimus," informed the page. "Just two days ago Gorsbenor sent away the last of the scullery maids. 'Tis only Karloff, Pudgett, the guards, and me. And every last landowner, peasant, and merchant is gone as well"

"What? Why?" blurted Terrence incredulously. The Ozians were disturbed to see yet another look of despair crossing the knight's handsome features. "Where," he squeaked in a tight voice, "where did he send them?"

The boy shrugged his shoulders, still nervously eyeing the guests. "I do not know, sir. Mayhap they have been shipped off somewhere. Or... or worse."

"Worse?" asked Terrence, his eyes beginning to well up with tears. "No, do not think that." He gazed at the boy. "But why are you still here? Uncle has no affection for thee."

"I've been telling lies that you've been ill, cooped up here in your chamber, and that you need me to care for you. That is the only reason I am still here."

"I'm Dorothy," spoke up the princess, extending her hand.

Seeing that the prince might not readily introduce his guests because of his emotional state, the other children followed suit.

"Saladin," said Button Bright, smiling.

"I'm Betsy," said the taller girl, curtsying.

"I'm Mayre, but you can call me Trot," said the youngest.

"No... people..." murmured the prince in disappointment and disbelief. "How can that be? Who then is there for me to rule?" The prince sat on the side of his bed, sinking into piles of dark furs and blankets.

"Who are these people he's talking about?" asked Dorothy, placing a hand on Terrence's shoulder. She joined him on the bed, sliding on the soft furs. "Who are... what were their names? Karloff, Pudgett? Are they loyal?"

"Pudgett is the personal aid to Gorsbenor, and Karloff is the cook," answered Christian, speaking for the prince. "By the way, my name is Christian. You must be the Princess."

"I'm *a* princess," replied Dorothy, exchanging a

handshake with him. "We're from Oz. Terrence found us… oh goodness. What time is it?"

"Christian," interrupted Terrence as he recovered his princely composure, "help me out of the rest of this armor that I may enjoy the meal with my new friends with more ease." He rose, and the page assisted him in removing the cumbersome metal greaves, which seemed to have lost their luminescence once they arrived in Castle Flora. Once garbed simply in his royal tunic and trousers, Terrence and Christian pulled the table to the bed, as well as two chairs and a stool, and the six seated themselves at the repast.

"Umm," hemmed Trot hesitantly, "do you have any water or juice or milk?" She looked in dismay at the wine as Christian filled a goblet of it for Terrence.

"Oh, of course," laughed Christian, setting the carafe on the table with a thump. "I won't be but a moment." He dashed behind the bookshelf and down the tunnel without so much as a backward glance. Curious, Button Bright looked after him, gazing in wonder at the tunnel opening behind the shelf.

Just as the five friends were about to eat a helping of bread and cheese, a thunderous noise filled the air and the doors of Terrence's chamber bulged inward. The table shook as the thunders repeated, and the bolt began to whine and bend.

"Get up! Hide!" hissed Terrence, rising to shield the children with his own body. A large battering ram suddenly shattered Terrence's door, showering the floor beneath it with the broken bolt and wood splinters, at the very moment the shelf clicked quietly into place, hiding the servant's tunnel.

"*Three* princesses, Terrence?" sneered a heavy man

entering amidst the debris. He waved his hand at four of the burly castle guards who immediately subdued Terrence, Betsy, Trot, and Dorothy. "'Twill do thee no good, boy. The kingdom, the castle, are mine, and so they shall remain." He gestured pompously at the guards. "Take them away from here!"

As the four were removed from the room, Dorothy could not help but notice, with mingled relief and worry, that Button Bright was nowhere to be found.

Chapter 6: The Secret Servant's Tunnel

BUTTON BRIGHT was always getting lost when he was younger. And in unfamiliar places it was quite easy for him to do so. But getting lost had its perks. Reverting to the old habit was like second nature to him. Whoever or whatever it was that came crashing through the door did not seem too friendly, and the secret servant's tunnel looked like a better prospect than facing the bearers of a battering ram.

The tunnel floor was smooth, he could feel that much. The walls were rounded, but rough. He could feel a layer of soot along the upper portion over his head, and wished that he had a torch with him. The Wizard's search-light was in Dorothy's dress pocket. It did him no good here and now. Still, the tunnel was closed off and the commotion was behind him. So were Dorothy, Betsy, Trot and Terrence. Button Bright winced, realizing that he left them in the lurch.

"Nothing to do about that now," he muttered,

slowly groping his way onward. He realized that the best course of action was to find a way out of this predicament, and then rescue his friends. No small task for a boy... at least, a boy who had lived as much life as he did. His demeanor belied his intelligence. Button Bright was a smart fellow, not to mention a Yookoohoo. "I bet Grandma Natch would have gotten us out of here by now. I suppose Ozma can't see us in the Magic Picture." He frowned, wishing his own ability had not been suppressed in this alternate realm. "Then again, maybe she might not."

The tunnel was not as dark as he thought. That, or his eyes were beginning to slowly acclimate to the dimness. He could make out the shape of the tunnel and its meandering path as it curved ahead of him. He could also see that the portion he was in was perfectly big enough for him to stand, so he arose and began striding forward. Shoving his hands into his pockets, he began to relax. "This isn't so bad," he thought.

He yawned, his jaw expanding mightily. "It *is* late," he muttered. The commotion from the room had subsided quickly, and he heard no indication of anyone entering the tunnel. Looking around for a smooth corner, Button Bright sat down, curled his legs to the side, and nestled his head in the crook of his arm. Despite his magic not functioning, Button Bright remained brave and secure. Yawning once more, he closed his eyes and decided to take a nap.

Ahead of him, Button Bright heard swift, light footsteps getting closer. Before he could even fall asleep, he was confronted by Christian, who was hurriedly making his way back to Terrence's chamber.

"Hello," he said as the two boys regarded each other in the dark tunnel, the jug of water Christian had brought sloshing its contents onto the floor.

Christian quickly set down the jug before much of the water was lost. "What was the commotion up there, master Saladin?" he asked of the boy. "Is something the matter?"

"That remains to be seen," replied Button Bright. "Something came crashing through the door, and next I knew I was in here looking for you."

"'Tis Gorsbenor," muttered the page under his breath. "He's come to remove Terrence for good. He desires only power, and eliminates those who stand in his way. The fool has even banished all the people he's supposed to rule over!" He looked imploringly at Button Bright. "Nor does he pay the guards more than a pittance. Mark my words: someday they will rebel against him and he will be doomed!"

"Weird," commented Button Bright, shaking his head. "That doesn't sound like the actions of a sane person to me!" He stretched, stood up, and arched his back. "Ugh. I'm tired."

"Come," urged Christian. "Let us see if they are still up there. Perhaps we..."

"Wait," said the other boy, placing a restraining hand on the page's shoulder. "Whoever barged into the room clearly wanted to remove us. They're not there now. Trust me. We need to figure out something else."

"We must go there anyway, to see *where* they've been taken. 'Tis obvious that they were taken prisoners!"

Button Bright failed to see the logic behind Christian's reason, but shrugged anyway. "Okay," he agreed, and followed him back to the bookshelf. Christian unhooked a latch, pushed the swinging shelf an inch outward and peered from behind it.

The table was covered with splinters of the broken door, and the oaken bolt lay shattered at the entrance to Terrence's chamber. The carafe of wine had spilled its contents onto the table and floor. There was no blood, for which both boys took heart. Christian pushed himself further out from behind the shelf and scrutinized the room.

"No one is here," he whispered to his companion. He pushed the bookshelf further open and stepped out from behind it, followed by Button Bright. "If I know Gorsbenor," he said, "he has probably put them in the dungeon until the next ship arrives at port. Then he will ship them off, though to where I cannot fathom."

"There's a port? I thought we were in the mountains."

"Aye, there is. Not far north is a bay, where Flora trades with other lands. All of our people either fled or were undoubtedly sent there."

"And when does that ship arrive?"

"There is another due on the morrow," replied Christian. "Mark my words: he will already begin to march the prisoners north this very night. Oh, many things have happened since Terrence went asearch of a princess!"

"That doesn't give us much time at all. So what do we do now?" asked Button Bright. He gazed at the floor, hoping to see if Dorothy might have dropped the Wizard's searchlight.

"That, children, is obvious," spoke a deep voice from the shattered doorway. The two boys whirled about to face the speaker as he emerged from the shadows.

"We must rescue the prince and his friends, then leave here as soon as we can," finished Necronimus with an assuring wink as he swept into the room. He surveyed the damage, then looked at the bookshelf. "And that is how we shall begin."

Necronimus swept past the boys and ducked behind the shelf. "Come!"

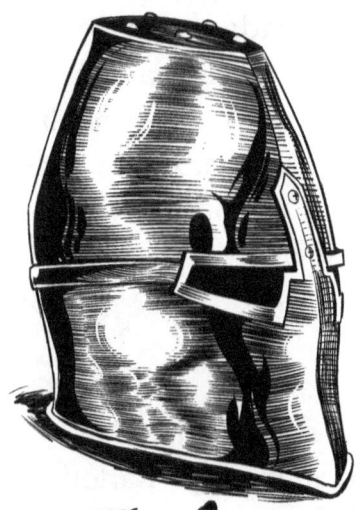

Chapter 7: Finding the Prisoners

THE THREE entered once more the tunnel, this time aided by the light of an old lamp that Necronimus produced from the folds of his robes.

"Shut that, boy," directed the wizard, ordering the page to secure the tunnel entrance.

Christian pulled the bookshelf securely closed behind them, and the three proceeded forward several yards before they stopped to huddle and discuss their options without being overheard by any guard lingering in a hallway or chamber.

"The guards are searching for both thee and me, boy," the wizard informed the page. He glared darkly at Christian, but the boy did not flinch underneath the heavy stare. "I do not believe they know of thy presence," he added to Button Bright, "but you appear to be in as much danger as we."

"Where do we go from here?" asked the boy from Oz. He shoved his hands in his pockets and stood still.

"This tunnel leads down to the kitchen," explained Christian slowly. "From there, if we can make it to the scullery, I know of another tunnel that leads down to the dungeons."

"By all means then," urged the wizard, "lead the way, boy!"

"This plan, however, is fraught with one slight danger," warned Christian ominously. "Karloff is loyal to Gorsbenor. What if we should run into him?"

"Who's Karloff?" asked Button Bright. He had heard the name before, but was not paying close attention.

"Karloff is the king's cook. We shall have to ford that stream when we come to it," replied Necronimus grimly. He reached into the pockets of his robes and took stock of what implements were available to him.

"I guess so," added Button Bright earnestly. "Lead on." He eyed the wizard guardedly. The old man was gloomy and dark, and not at all friendly and hopeful like Terrence and Christian. "You have a scary name, by the way," he said.

"Necronimus," said the wizard in response. "Yes, I suppose it is. Be assured, boy: I do not practice what the name indicates. It is one of many that I have adopted in this lifetime."

Christian looked at the old wizard in consternation. "That's not your name?" he asked.

"Oh, indeed it is," spoke the old man, smirking darkly. "But for other people, other places, my name is different. In the southern continent, where there are fell beasts and foul creatures, I am known as the Sonnenmench, Slayer of Mouroth." He produced a vision cupped in an outstretched hand, showing a brilliant miniature version of himself thrusting a lance through the breast of a terrifying dragon. "And in the west, I am known simply as Lathe, maker of wands and weaver of charms. In the north, I am the toymaker Klaus." He produced another glowing image of himself, garbed in red and white furs, handing toys to children in an area filled with snow-covered pine trees.

"These guises seem so different from you," marveled Christian. "When were these events?"

"Many lifetimes ago did I slay the beast, but you understand that I travel, young master Christian. I am Necronimus at this time, and I am also Klaus and Lathe."

Button Bright had heard of wizards that change their names and even their appearances. Zim Greenleaf, the flying sorcerer of Oz, went by many different names, and even appearances. This was not as startling to him as it was to the page. He felt better about the wizard, and smiled genially at the old man, who returned the favor. "So, then, why Necronimus? That's a Latin name, I think."

The wizard glowered. "Yes, it was a name given to me... in recognition of services I provided for Gorsbenor when I first came to his employ."

"Something to do with the dead," persisted Button Bright. He felt he knew where the conversation as going, but wanted the old man to elaborate.

"Animator of the dead."

Christian paled, and looked agog at the wizard. "Wh-what?"

Necronimus returned the child's look, then cast his eyes down. "I have done things for Terrence's uncle that I am not proud of. I cannot undo the past, but I can work to make things right." He looked meaningfully through narrowed eyes at the boys, then nodded for them to continue.

The trek through the castle walls to the kitchen was uneventful. Christian used the passageway often enough to maintain its cleanliness and upkeep. He explained that when the castle was constructed many centuries ago, the builders included the tunnels to spy on the king and try to extort money from him. However their efforts turned out, the tunnels were eventually covered up and forgotten until he stumbled upon them by accident.

Button Bright scraped his right knee on some of the stones that made up the tunnel, for at one point all three had to crawl on hands and knees to get through a particularly narrow section. The entire journey took less than ten minutes, and Necronimus doused the lamp when Christian informed them that they neared the kitchen.

"Hold a moment," said the boy. He held his hand upon a large slab of rock that looked too impossibly heavy for a child his size to handle. "It is no longer hot. Good." It swung easily on a hinge, revealing the inner walls of a vast oven. He gingerly knelt down and touched the floor and walls of the oven. "It is safe. Come."

Christian slowly crawled from the tunnel into the oven, then pushed open the oven door to look out into the kitchen. Seeing no one, he quietly pushed the oven door all the way open and emerged, followed by Button Bright and Necronimus. The old wizard was surprisingly nimble for his apparent age.

"Well, we're here," observed Button Bright as he emerged from the oven, "and I don't see any cook." The kitchen was brightly lit with at least three lamps and two sputtering torches. Bowls of meats and loaves of bread were arrayed on the cook-tops, and flies buzzed around their heads, hopping around on the food items. "Ugh," he grimaced in distaste, sneering at the unappealing food.

"All the better," hissed Necronimus, putting his finger to his lips for silence. He whispered to the page, "Show us where that other passageway is, Christian." He shuffled swiftly to the doorway separating the kitchen from the scullery.

"It is this way..." began the page before his voice trailed off. He stood next to the wizard, and was about to push open the kitchen door when it was opened inward upon them.

A fat, burly man emerged from the scullery, carrying with him a greasy hock of lamb and a large cleaver. He wore a white hat upon his head that Button Bright almost laughed at. "That looks exactly like a chef's hat!" he thought to himself.

"Well, well," spoke the cook with a smug grin on his face. "And what might the three of thee be doing in mine own kitchen?" He blocked the frame of the door with his vast size, holding his ground. "Hungry, are we?"

"Oh, well... Karloff..." hedged Christian nervously. He backed up closer to Necronimus, hoping to get lost in the wizard's vast robes. "We are here to... umm..."

"We are here to ask of thee a favor," interrupted Necronimus. "We know Gorsbenor is searching for us, and we would prefer to keep our skins on our backs. We need for thee to allow us to offer him an... er... a meal. As a peace offering, you see. We would have him think highly of us, as of you for preparing it, of course." Necronimus knew very well that the cook was extremely slow and stupid, even as a master gourmand, and hoped that his obvious—and ridiculous—lies would not fall on deaf ears.

Christian looked around the cook at Button Bright. "Master Saladin! Please. Master Karloff prepares food on that."

The cook turned to glance at Button Bright, who was crawling on the counter top behind him, apparently stacking dishes.

"The boy is helpful. Ha ha!" he laughed. "Leave him be. As for this meal you wish... Do not think that thou wilst coerce me to prepare it," grunted the cook as he bit off a piece of the mutton chop, "Not I. And if anyone should find thee in my kitchen, Gorsbenor would have my hide as well!" The large man screwed his face into a knot, thinking so hard that the fleas were forced to vacate his heated cranium. "No, I will have to tell Gorsbenor mysel—"

His sentence was cut short by a cast-iron frying pan as it made contact with the back of his head. It was not enough to cause the cook to lose consciousness, but as he turned to face his attacker, another pan, wielded by the wizard, finished the job.

"How could you be so reckless, Saladin?" The page decided not to dwell on Button Bright's risky behavior. He stepped over the prone form obstructing the doorway.

"Come quickly!" urged Christian as the three entered the scullery. "We must get to the dungeon before he awakens!"

The other two clambered over Karloff and entered the scullery. Piles of dirty dishes were stacked everywhere they could see. Heaps of soiled clothes beset the room as well, and vermin scurried about—rats, hundreds of cockroaches, and swarms of flies. Button Bright struggled to control his reaction to gag.

Christian grabbed a torch from its sconce by the door, deftly moved around piles of dirty clothes and pulled open two cupboard doors at the rear of the room. He then removed several boxes from within, and swept the open space with the torch, scattering vermin from their path. He then clambered into the cupboard, followed by

Necronimus with his lantern, and finally Button Bright, who closed the cupboard doors behind him.

The tunnel behind the cupboard was less hospitable than the previous, for though Christian knew of it, he had explored it only once, long before. Cobwebs, dust, and various scraps of unidentifiable waste littered the crumbling structure, and the three had to be especially careful, lest they hurt themselves or cause a racket that draw attention to themselves. Rats and cockroaches scuttled about them, making the journey even more uncomfortable. In no time at all, they were able to stand upright, and Necronimus shone his lantern to guide their way.

The tunnel carved a downward slope into the mountain top, and the air grew more stale, heavier, wet and cold. The sound of water dripping blended with the sound of rats and the scurrying of roaches. Several times they found themselves slipping on the wet rock, scattering tunnel debris.

"It's not much further," commented Christian. He and the others were short on breath from their efforts and the dank tunnel air. A foul stench wafted up from side tunnels and from deep crevices in the tunnel floor, over which they had to step.

A sound echoed from one of the side tunnels.

"Must be the wind," mumbled Christian, faltering and causing the others to pause behind him.

"What's down that way?" asked Button Bright quietly, peering off into the pitch darkness of one of the tunnels.

The wizard sucked in a quick breath, then answered for the page. "The catacombs lie down there," he said. "Terrence and Gorsbenor's forebears sleep there."

"But what was that sound?" insisted Button Bright. "How can it be the wind? Aren't we inside a mountain or something?"

The wizard held the lamp outward toward a tunnel, casting dark shadows around him. "Gorsbenor assigned monks to guard the dead," he spoke. "Many, many moons ago. I do not know how they fare. I am forbidden to give them aid or food."

"Mireille used to do that," offered Christian, wrinkling his nose in distaste. "She was... a strange one."

Still inquisitive, Button Bright resumed his barrage of questions. "What happened to her? And why did she want to hurt Terrence? And his dog?"

"Mireille met her end the night she ended Angus' life," retorted the wizard hotly. "I did what was best for the prince. I protected him. I avenged his..." He realized how futile his statements were—justifying the murder of a person in retaliation for her misdeeds. He bit his lip and grew silent. Calming himself, Necronimus slowed his breathing and leveled his gaze ahead of himself. "I took Mireille's life. That, too, is a deed that I regret and wish to absolve myself of." He turned to Button Bright, his eyes stern. "You asked why she chose to hurt the prince. That is because she was in Gorsbenor's employ, and sought only to please herself. Hers were selfish desires. His uncle promised her riches if she would eliminate Terrence. She was ineffectual, and succeeded only in killing the dog."

Striding forward as he spoke, the wizard continued. "It was to protect the prince from her that I killed her. She was evil, yet I regret having to take such actions. It seems I continue to do things that would make me a bad wizard, and not a good one."

Button Bright wanted to console the old man, for he felt that the wizard was genuinely sorry for his deeds. The boy could not find the right words to say, so he kept silent. The wizard appeared to be good, but by his own admission he committed some truly dark deeds. His lungs hurt from the dank air, and the oppressive tunnel seemed to be closing in on him.

"I'm not afraid to admit I'm a little scared," he muttered. As if to punctuate his statement, another moan wafted up from the catacombs below. Instinctually, Button Bright reached out and grasped Necronimus' hand. The wizard, taken aback but heartened by the child's display of trust, grasped his hand warmly, and smiled in assurance. "We will be in the dungeons soon. I will do my best to protect you." He addressed Christian. "Both of you. Be brave, my boys."

They continued to trek downward in the greasy, dark tunnel. When Christian was uncertain of the way to go, the wizard took the lead. "I know these tunnels," he spoke softly. "For I have used them. Come with me."

After walking with the wizard a distance, Button Bright spoke again. "Can I ask you one more thing?"

The old man turned softened eyes to the boy, grateful that Button Bright was making the effort to reach him. The levels of protection that the wizard had cloaked about himself were beginning to peel away, and he felt he could relieve some of the stress of his own existence by answering his questions. "Please, ask," he answered kindly.

"Why is Gorsbenor doing this? Why is he getting rid of people? You said something about an army? I'm not sure I understand. What's the sense in getting rid of the people if he's going to build an army?"

Necronimus chuckled. "That's more than just *one thing*," he said quietly. He nodded. "Gorsbenor sought my aid in building an army that he could control without question. He wanted an invincible force that would allow him to conquer any... opponent he might encounter. I believe it is his intent to situate himself as ruler of our entire realm. And to do that, he needs to employ certain *unconventional* means."

Seeing that Button Bright was easily following his words, but that Christian appeared perplexed, Necronimus elaborated. "Gorsbenor wishes to conquer as much as his mind will allow. To do that, he has enticed me to animate the bodies of the dead, to serve him blindly as a mindless army. I... I did his bidding, at first. But the longer I worked for Gorsbenor, the more I realized the madness and... the *evil* of his intentions. That is why I have chosen to serve Terrence, and to aid him. There is nothing left for the prince here. Perhaps... perhaps there is something for him elsewhere."

Button Bright smiled hopefully at the wizard.

The tunnel began to level out and there were more pebbles and dust gathered about their feet. The sounds of far off moans began to fade, though their effect was still terrifying for all three. Their lungs hurt from the dank air and their shoulders hurt from the cramped tunnel and the stress they found themselves under. For a tunnel that was supposed to be shorter than the servant's tunnel, the tunnel to the dungeon proved to be much more of a task. Christian put his finger to his lips and put out his torch by grinding it against the tunnel floor. He dropped it down by their feet so that the smoke would not creep out into the dungeon. Necronimus dimmed his lantern, and the three crept toward a flat slab of wood that blocked their exit.

The page unlatched several hooks and a bolt, then pushed with all his might against the slab. Button Bright and Necronimus joined him, and the three were soon able to budge the slab from their path. A rattling noise from the other side of the door stopped them cold, but after waiting a moment and hearing nothing else, they continued to push, taking care to ease it slowly. Something on the other side of the slab was loose, and the slightest jolt would cause a small cacophony.

A sliver of pale light met their eyes, and they could see a torch out beyond the slab. Upon emergence from, of all places, behind the key rack in the dungeon, they were relieved to discover that the rattling keys had not woken the slumbering guard.

Three stealthy intruders quietly scurried into the main room of the castle dungeon, carefully withdrawing a ring of keys from the wall that they had just moved. Not wanting to make any further noise, they elected to leave the slab ajar. The single guard in the entry was fast asleep, and snoring deeply.

Christian led his two companions past the seated guard and through a doorway which was thankfully unlocked. The oaken door swung open with a creak, and all three froze. But the guard remained undisturbed. Beyond that was a hallway dotted with barred chambers.

"Dungeons," whispered Christian, though it was obvious to Button Bright and Necronimus what they viewed.

There was no way of knowing the lateness of the hour. The only wakeful person that they encountered was Karloff the cook, and he could have been awake early to prepare the king's breakfast, or up late. All that they knew for sure was that their time was limited, and they needed to find their companions. Without wasting any time, they dashed down the dungeon hallway, peering into the darkened cells. With luck, the very first cell proved to contain Prince Terrence and the others.

Necronimus whispered harshly. "My prince! Awaken! We must be away from here!"

Within the dungeon, four figures stirred, rubbing grimy sleep from their eyes. The sound of keys being tried in the lock alerted them that there was someone at the door. Despite the pitch darkness, the light from an ensconced torch in the hallway showed them all that they needed to see.

"Button Bright!" whispered Dorothy, Trot, and Betsy gleefully, pressing themselves against the rusty iron bars of the holding cell they were in.

"Christian! Necronimus!" whispered Terrence from the same cell. "Can you get us out of here?"

"We are working on it," replied the old wizard, frowning in concentration. He continued to try the ring of keys at the cell entrance and in no time at all had the four captives free.

"But we are not out of danger yet," reminded Christian, pointing back to the dungeon entrance. The guard was still sleeping.

"Come quickly," Necronimus whispered. "We must go back to my tower. We can devise an escape from there." Gliding on silent feet, all seven of them dashed to the dungeon entrance, past the sleeping guard, and into the tunnel behind the key rack.

"We run the risk of encountering Karloff, or worse, once we get to the scullery," muttered Necronimus angrily. There was no way around that. It was an obstacle that they would be forced to face.

"We cannot stop now," said Terrence. "What other options have we?"

All were in agreement. The seven entered the tunnel once more, shutting it with a click and soft rattle of keys behind them.

"Eh?" mumbled the guard as he leaned his head against the far wall of the dungeon. He closed his eyes again wearily and went back to sleep.

Chapter 8: Escape to the Wizard's Tower

THE tunnel leading from the dungeon branched into separate directions not more than twenty paces in. Christian had retrieved the torch he had set down, and lit it again from the wizard's lantern. He offered it to Terrence, who took it silently.

Logically, the group of people chose the largest tunnel, which led upward. Despite the darkness and fear, the children kept tight-lipped and obedient, following Necronimus and Christian. Terrence brought up the rear. The only sound to be heard was the crackling of the torch as the flame burned away at the pitch.

The wizard slowed his forward motion, then came to a stop. As the others stopped behind him, he turned to address them.

"We have taken a wrong turn," he said, looking back apologetically at them.

"How can you be sure?" asked Christian. "There was only one way to go. We're going up." He paused, looking frantically at the wizard. "Aren't... we...?"

Betsy gasped and drew Trot close to her. The girls shivered in the cold tunnel, and fought to keep their breathing controlled.

"What is going on?" demanded Dorothy, her own teeth chattering. A howl of despair carried up from the depths of the tunnel, sending the hairs on the backs of all their necks to stand on end. The princess stifled a shriek, and covered her mouth with her hand. Her eyes widened as she shot a look of terror at the prince and his companions. "What... what was that? Please. What was that?"

"We have to get out of here," insisted Trot as tears beginning to trickle down her cheeks. She clung closer to Betsy.

Necronimus reached into a pocket of his robes. He pulled out a satchel of powder, and handed his lamp to Button Bright. "Please hold this, my boy," he said, his brow furrowed with unease.

As Button Bright held the lamp up, they could all see Necronimus emptying an amount of powder into his hand. Stashing the cloth satchel back into a pocket, the wizard cupped both hands together before his lips, then blew the powder against the tunnel wall.

As the powder settled, a vision appeared before their eyes. Everywhere the powder touched the wall of the tunnel there appeared hand prints that glowed bright white in the light of the lantern. The prints were scattered all over the tunnel wall, and many of them smeared in the direction they were walking. Everywhere they looked, the smears appeared to drip downward, and they could see, now revealed in the lantern light, streams of blood and ichor along the floor of the tunnel.

Dorothy gasped, at a loss for words. Such a sight was not something she had ever encountered before. But she knew, in her heart, that the life-blood of unfortunate people had bled out in these tunnels. Her face turned downward. "Wh-what happened here?" she started to ask, but was unable to continue.

At the rear of the entourage, Terrence glanced at the tunnel walls, and saw a most disheartening sight. Though the powder did not show hand prints where he squatted, the prince saw instead fingernails embedded into crevices on the tunnel wall, indicating where people had struggled to their last to pull away from whatever had dragged them down there. He choked back a sob, stretching his face out in a silent cry.

"We must retrace our steps," spoke the wizard, his voice cracking. "Come. Children, come with me. My prince, let us go." Necronimus gingerly stepped past the huddled forms of Dorothy, Betsy and Trot, once again extending his hand to Button Bright. The boy returned the lantern to him as they doubled back.

"Come on," Button Bright urged to the girls as he and Christian stepped past them. "We need to go."

Nodding, Dorothy managed to gather her wits as best she could and swallowed audibly. "C-come on," she said to Trot and Betsy. She reached her hands to the girls, pulling them along. "We... we'll be out of here soon enough. Then we can all go home."

"B-but..." began Trot, asked quietly. "Why doesn't Ozma bring us back *now*? What's taking her so long? The Magic Picture..."

Dorothy shook her head. "I don't know. I just don't know."

"She can't see us," said Betsy, her face long and drawn. "Don't you realize that? If she could see us, she'd have gotten us out of here long ago. But she can't see us. And that means she can't help us. We are on our own!" Betsy's voice echoed down the tunnels.

As if in answer to her, a symphony of wails reverberated up from the tunnel's depths.

"Be silent," stated the wizard. He whirled around, almost knocking Christian over the head with his lantern as he did so. He froze in his spot, and the others did the same.

Necronimus did not move; rather, his eyes darted around to regard the children and the prince gathered around him. They were relying on him to lead them out of their predicament, and he knew that it was his duty to lead them to safety.

The wizard closed his eyes, allowing the spots of color that the torch and lantern had burned into his retinas to waver in and out of vision. Pursing his lips, he began to slow his breathing until his heart began to beat regularly. The wailing continued, but lessened somewhat. Letting out a breath, he spoke.

"The nature of my business with Gorsbenor is foul indeed. *Was* foul. I am no longer in his employ, nor have I been for some time. But because I am responsible for what we are about to encounter—if indeed we do—then I must warn you that... what we might see... will be *unpleasant*."

"What will we see?" asked Terrence in a small, quiet voice.

"The dead, my prince," replied the old man, hanging his head in shame. He raised his eyes to face Terrence. "We shall see the dead. We shall see Gorsbenor's army."

Dorothy said the only sensible thing she could think to. "Oh, I do hope we don't. Please, let's... let's just leave. Do you have a way to bring us home?"

Licking his lips, Necronimus nodded. "Come."

The wizard led them swiftly back down the tunnel to where it branched off, and there they paused. Button Bright regarded the dust and grime on the floor of the tunnel, and could just make out enough scrapes to determine which tunnel they had come down from.

"The catacombs are where he is building his army," mumbled Necronimus to no one in particular, though Button Bright tightened his grip on the old man's hand. "The people... have not truly been sent away. They are still here."

"You should not have gong alone with him," said Christian sternly, casting an angry glare at the wizard.

"I know," was all the old wizard said, and led the way out. Unseen by the others, Necronimus snarled in disgust, then quickly flattened his lips into an emotionless mask of stern indifference.

PUDGETT, tapping his toe in annoyance, was waiting for them as they emerged from the cupboard. Pudgett was an ugly fellow, rather portly and balding, with piggish eyes and a look of putrid contempt upon his sickly face. He had been staring at the cupboard and turned in surprise when the escapees emerged from behind a shelf instead.

"And what, pray tell," he sneered in a nasally voice as first Necronimus, then Christian and Button Bright emerged, "didst thou find in that cupboard? I knew all along," continued the steward without waiting for an explanation, "that there were secret tunnels in here. Now you've proven it!" He began to laugh in a manner that seemed more like hyperventilating.

"Master Pudgett," laughed Christian nervously, closing the tunnel entry door with his foot before Terrence or the others could emerge. Thankfully, the others had heard the unfamiliar voice and remained silent. "Thou... Thou dost

70

not want to go in there. There's... rats! Hordes of rats! I tell thee, Karloff's kitchen is very unsanitary!"

"Oh?" replied Pudgett in mock disbelief, "then that is why he is lying on the kitchen floor. Food poisoning... or maybe even the plague!" he added in sarcasm. "Why does not our resident wizard here enchant them and turn all those rats into nice pastries for the king and me, hmmm?" He knew full well of the vermin that infested the castle kitchen. The thought of improper sanitation did not disturb him.

"You are blind. He is using you. Gorsbenor is no king," growled Christian darkly under his breath.

"Oh? And I suppose thy Sir Terrence is? Mayhaps he is in the tunnel. I think I shall just have a look." Pudgett pushed the three aside, not without a good deal of resistance from them, and reached out to pull the shelf aside. "Apparently there is more than one entrance to this tunnel, eh?"

The shelf flew outward suddenly as Terrence emerged in a rage, knocking the steward backward and unto the dirty floor, sending a stack of pots and pans that were atop the shelf flying.

"I would not want to be king of such a barren keep as this is anyway, sniveling worm!" he shouted. "There is nothing left for me here. Gorsbenor has my blessings if he wishes to rule an empty castle and a barren land!"

Pudgett lay sprawled upon the floor, shaking and rubbing his head. "Leave me alone!" he gurgled sheepishly as he groggily rose. "Leave me alone or I shall tell the king! Ohh... my head! You made me hit my head!"

"Simpering buffoon," said Necronimus. "Gorsbenor is not king. What *king* would rid the land of the very people he wishes to rule? Does he wish to work the fields and tend animals on his own? He is touched in the head. Thou must be a fool to serve such a madman!"

"That does it!" cried the stumbling Pudgett as he turned to the door. "Let us see what he thinks of being called a madman!"

"Let him go," spoke Necronimus calmly, placing his hand on Terrence's shoulder to prevent the prince from following. "He shan't get far." Necronimus waved his hands in the air and chanted an archaic spell. "*Tu lo sai*, Pudgett, *tu draco, sai lo tu*," he spoke. A figure formed in the space of air between them and the door; that of a fierce green dragon much like the one he had conjured earlier. "He is positively terrified of them," sneered the wizard as the illusion passed through the door and began pursuing the cowardly steward. A scream of terror was soon heard somewhat further down the corridor. "It would be comical if the situation was not so dire," sighed the wizard, turning to the others.

"Their noise will alert the guards," cried Dorothy in exasperation as she looked out from behind the shelf. "Why did you do that?"

"Worry not, my dear," chortled the old wizard, assisting her to emerge. "They are

quite accustomed to Pudgett and his screams. It is what little amusement the men can afford here."

"I certainly hope so," said Dorothy dubiously. "His screams could wake the Wicked Witch of the South!"

"They are still asleep," reassured Necronimus mysteriously. "Have no fear." He winked, noting the girl's quizzical look.

"Come on out! Hurry!" called Christian urgently to the two girls remaining in the tunnel. Trot and Betsy emerged looking somewhat ruffled but none the worse for wear.

"Lead us now to my chamber," commanded Terrence of the page as he grasped the boy's shoulders. "Then we shall flee to Necronimus' tower!"

"Have a care," responded Christian tersely, looking over his shoulder in the direction of Pudgett's departure. "We may not be so safe yet!" He led the entourage from the scullery to the kitchen, around Karloff's still-unconscious form, and directly to the vast oven.

"You're leading us into a stove?" gasped Trot fearfully.

"The fire's out, milady," said Christian without bothering to look back at her. He opened the large oven door and was about to step in when he froze in place.

"What's the matter?" asked Betsy Bobbin anxiously. "What's going on?" She sidled close to the boy and peered into the empty stove.

"Sshh! Listen!" hissed the page angrily, indicating the tunnel beyond the back wall of the oven.

"...looks like people have been here..." came one voice from deep within its bowels.

"...tell the king..." trailed another voice, its echoes reverberating within the vast stove as they reached the companions' ears.

"They've discovered my tunnels!" cried Christian in mottled anger and frustration. "Gorsbenor must have sent them to find me. I don't know *how* they discovered the bookcase..."

"The trail of water," mumbled Necronimus in dismay. "Thou left a trail of water behind thee from the water jug, and it disappeared behind the bookcase. The guards are not *that* dim."

"That matters little now," muttered Terrence to his friends. To the rest of the companions he ventured, "We must somehow reach Necronimus' tower. The only way from here is to walk—or run—directly along the hallways leading to the ante-room."

"But won't the castle be crawling with guards?" inquired Trot fearfully of the three castle regulars. "Can't we just barricade ourselves in here?"

"My magicks are limited compared to the sorcerers of your world," admitted Necronimus. "I do have some skill, however, that skill is tied to implements that are too cumbersome to keep on my person. We must get to my tower."

"'Tis entirely possible that we may not even encounter the guards," answered the prince, though his words did little to comfort his companions... nor himself. He realized the improbability of his statement, but said no more.

"I will take that chance," announced the wizard bravely. "Some of the men fear me, and I do have some tricks I can use to foil them... or at least *try* to."

"All right," directed Dorothy, "let's go then. And please hurry! The sooner we get out of here the happier I'll be."

Christian fearfully peered out of the kitchen door to the empty hallway beyond and waved the others to follow through. Necronimus' shuffling feet led the way, followed by Dorothy, Button Bright, Betsy, Christian, and Trot. Terrence fell to the rear, protective of his newfound friends.

They had made great progress, and as Necronimus informed them, were almost to the ante-room when shouts of alarm and outrage were heard from behind and below them.

"The prince has escaped!"

"Pudgett says he saw his bratty page and the wizard!"

"They're heading for the tower!"

"Hurry!" ordered Christian, almost in a panic. He dashed forward past the others to open the ante-room door and herd the rest of them out into the early morning air. Beside the castle entry they saw a flight of stone stairs that rose through the air to meet the base of a tower situated on a nearby mountain crag. The stairs were held up by sturdy wooden beams, but still looked precarious.

"Let's go!" cried Trot, bravely running out of the castle toward the base of the steps. "We can make it! Come on!"

"Oh my," gasped Betsy, following her friend.

"There they are!" shouted a guard from the far end of the hallway, seeing Terrence and Christian vanish into the ante-room. Their clattering footfalls resounded as the guards dashed up to the door.

Terrence bolted the door behind them and leaned his weight against it as Necronimus led the five children out on the stairway.

"Come prince!" urged the old wizard into the ante-room to Terrence, who was straining to hold back the rattling and bulging door. "They will have the battering ram soon. Thou cannot hold against that!"

"Go! I will follow!" ordered Terrence through his clenched teeth. Necronimus dashed up the swaying steps and joined the others as they trekked to the base of his tower.

"Come Terrence!" he called across the open space to the castle. "Thou cannot hold them off much longer! Hurry!"

Like a bolt of lightning the companions witnessed Terrence dash from the ante-room out onto the precarious steps and up the steps to the tower. Behind him several guards were heard smashing at the door.

All seven of them climbed the stone stairway as fast as they could, and made it to the base of the wizard's tower.

To their surprise, Necronimus, in a display of superhuman strength, picked up the slab of rock that composed the top step and hurled it at the center of the stairway. With a thunderous clatter, the unstable structure that connected the castle and tower fell shattered to the ground far below.

Chapter 10: To Oz

"**WE ARE TRAPPED** here like birds in a cage," muttered Christian darkly. "I pray thou art able to take us away from here," he said to Necronimus.

Winds outside the tower pushed against the structure, causing it to sway precariously. Now that the stone stairwell was no more, it had nothing to fortify it, so the tower began to move awkwardly.

"There is an immediate escape," said the wizard to the assembled group within the horrifyingly swaying tower. "And there is another that would take more time than we have and more ingredients than are housed within my tower." As he spoke, the older gentleman bustled about the tower, gathering packets and vials and piling them into a crucible situated on a table in the center of the tower room.

"Tell us!" pleaded Dorothy, following him and nearly treading on the hem of his robes.

The wizard, though visibly exhausted from his unbelievable display of power, spoke clearly and precisely, "The four of you belong in Oz. I shall have no problem in returning you, but Terrence, Christian, and I are from this time and place, and ours would not be a complete journey to your land."

"What exactly dost thou mean?" inquired the page sternly of the elder gentleman. He was propping himself up against one of the tower walls, watching the wizard and Dorothy move about.

Necronimus stopped his movement and glared at the page. "Terrence, thee and I would arrive in the land of Oz in incorporeal forms. We would be there in existence, but our bodies would have little—if any—physical substance."

"You'd be like ghosts!" breathed Betsy in horror.

"Oh no," whispered Tiny Trot sympathetically as she noted the anxious expressions on Christian's and Terrence's faces. She moved closer to Betsy and clung to her friend's arm.

All eyes turned to regard the prince.

"I have nothing left here to rule over even if I *did* become king," said Terrence in a trembling voice. "What am I a prince of if all my people and my friends have been taken away?" He dropped his head and ran his fingers through his long hair. "Life as a ghost may not be too appealing right now, but I pray that it is better than what may befall us should we remain here." He chuckled mirthlessly. "I fear we would all become ghosts then."

"My place is by my friend and liege," said Christian, puffing out his chest and setting his chin. "I go where Terrence goes."

Necronimus regarded the two, and thought about his many lives. Closing his eyes, he spoke. "As do I," sighed the wizard with resignation. "I am a fugitive now, as are my two friends."

"I'm sure Ozma or Glinda or the Wizard of Oz can give you real bodies," Dorothy told them, giving them some comfort.

"They're really powerful magicians," added Betsy, adding fuel to their resolution. "You see! It won't be bad at all! They're the most powerful magicians ever! They'll fix you all up in a jiffy!"

"Yeah," said Trot, "and they... whoa!"

A tremendous jolt sent all seven companions flying through the air to the floor of the tower.

"What was that?" demanded Button Bright excitedly

as he picked himself up and helped Dorothy and Trot to rise.

"The guards!" shouted Terrence fearfully. "They are trying to topple the tower!" Another jolt rocked the tower before he could peer out the window to confirm his suspicions. "If you are going to take us away from here, master Necronimus," he cried, "do it now!"

A third jolt caused the walls of the tower to begin crumbling as the old wizard bent to retrieve a gnarled wooden staff that had fallen to the floor amidst several other magical artifacts.

The crucible he had been clutching to his chest was set on the floor and he tapped the rim of it with his staff.

"Cursum Perficio," he began, waving the magic wand mystically in the air before them, and tossing it back and forth in his hands. A light began to emanate from the staff, slowly enveloping the room and its occupants.

"Cursum Perficio,
Verbum Sapienti.
Quo plus habent,
eo plus cupiunt.
Post Nubila Phoebus,
Post Nubila Phoebus,
Post Nubila Phoebus,
Iternum, Iternum, Iternum!"

And the walls of the stone tower came tumbling down.

Chapter 11:
Back in Ozma's Palace

"**G**OOD heavens, dear children!" exclaimed Glinda uncharacteristically. "Where in creation have you been?"

"And why are there now *three* ghosts?" asked Ozma incredulously, seeing the three disembodied spirits who accompanied their sudden reappearance in the now brightly-lit reading room.

"Oh, Ozma!" cried Dorothy, hugging her dear friend tightly. "We've been in a dark castle and a dungeon and an oven and secret tunnels, and we've been chased and shook up and scared out of our wits, and..."

Dorothy went on to explain their entire adventure to Ozma, Glinda, and the Wizard, aided by Trot, Betsy and Button Bright. They were joined by Polychrome and Scraps, who were both greatly relieved to see their friends unharmed.

"And these are our new friends Prince Terrence, Christian, and Necronimus," finished Dorothy, indicating the three ghosts who were nervously standing beside her. She gravely faced Ozma. "They're here to stay."

"Well, I'm glad to *finally* meet you," said Ozma to Prince Terrence. She addressed all three: "I welcome all of you to my land. It gives me great pleasure to provide you refuge from your dire troubles."

"The pleasure is all ours," replied Terrence in a barely audible voice as he kneeled gallantly before Ozma. The troubled look upon his face reappeared, disconcerting Dorothy, who felt that he should have been relieved.

"What's the matter, Terrence?" she asked. "Everything will be all right."

"Oh, Ozma," cut in Trot, "do you think you and Glinda and the Wiz could give them their bodies back? Dorothy kind of promised them that you would."

"It's not that," interjected Terrence. "I just feel that... well, all I've done is ask and take, and yet you freely give..."

The little queen looked to her advisors. "This is highly unusual. What do you think?"

"Well, we certainly can *try*," stated Glinda calmly, "But Necronimus must know that practicing magic is forbidden in Oz to any others except to whom special permission has been granted by the Queen."

"I am more than happy to give up that troublesome craft," acquiesced Necronimus with a bow. "I was not such a good wizard anyway."

"Then let us waste no time in restoring their true forms!" said Ozma with a smile. "Oscar, I trust you and Glinda will take care of the details while we prepare for the luncheon?"

"Of course, my friend," replied Oscar Diggs, returning her knowing smile. "I shall do my best, as always."

"Oh! Jinnicky," said Ozma, in an afterthought. "You and he work very well together. I shall contact him and ask him to help."

The Wizard's smile threatened to crack, but he maintained his pleasant demeanor. "Of *course*, dear Ozma. I would dearly love to see our old friend again."

The Patchwork Girl, very familiar with the Wizard's distaste for his rival from across the Deadly Desert, laughed "Hah!" and stuck out her tongue, before somersaulting around the room and right through Christian, Terrence, and Necronimus.

"Oh! Stop!" cried Polychrome, distressed to see the

three disembodied spirits dissipate, then slowly reform.

"Scraps! Stop that this instant!" declared Ozma sternly. She was relieved to see their three guests looking none the worse for wear, but still was vexed with the life-sized ragdoll.

Calling her attention away from the Patchwork Girl, Glinda spoke. "Zim Greenleaf is in town, visiting the arboretum he set up in the royal gardens. He has experience regenerating lost limbs and restoring entire bodies." The sorceress smiled in confidence. "Recall how much he has benefitted our dear Nick Chopper, as well as the great Tititi Hoochoo."

Ozma was familiar with how Zim had given the Tin Woodman the ability to switch from his tin body to his original body of flesh at will. She was glad that Nick often chose to retain his customary tin body, but was grateful that he had been given the freedom to choose. The Private Citizen, Tititi Hoochoo, had his missing heart regenerated by the same sorcerer.

"Have Jellia prepare three extra seats for our guests," advised Glinda as she left Ozma and the adventurers. "Whether we are swift in our work or not, we cannot have them miss the celebration." She addressed the ghostly visitors. "We will send for you as soon as we have made progress."

"Lunch? Dinner?" queried Betsy Bobbin, rubbing her stomach. "Just how long have we been gone?"

"Since late last night, of course!" replied Ozma, smiling again. "You missed breakfast!" She addressed at the assemblage. "Why don't the four of you take a nap and get cleaned up. It seems like you could use some rest."

Ozma ushered the children, Scraps, and the Rainbow's

daughter from the reading room. She smiled assuringly at them as they left, then turned her attention to Terrence, Necronimus, and Christian.

"Necronimus is an unusual name," Ozma said to the ghostly wizard.

"I go by others, as well. I am particularly fond of the name Klaus. I have many happy memories with it."

Ozma nodded. "Klaus it shall be then." She extended her hands to the three ghosts. "Please, keep me company until Glinda calls for you."

The celebrities, gathered in the grand banquet hall of Ozma's palace, rose from their seats to greet the Wizard, Glinda, a tall, lanky man with a grand plume of green hair, and a short, smiling man encased in a red jar as they made their way to the head of the grand table, along with the three people they led into the room.

"Good citizens of Oz, friends," announced Ozma, "please give a royal welcome to our newest Emerald Citizens: Terrence of Flora, Christian, and Klaus the toymaker!"

A roar of cheers and applause welcomed them to the luncheon, where they took their seats near the head of the table, alongside Dorothy, Button Bright, Trot, and Betsy.

"Klaus," echoed Button Bright. "I like that."

Polychrome, the Rainbow's daughter, cast an innocent smile at Sir Terrence, then blushed as the former knight returned her gesture.

The Patchwork Girl, on the other hand, stuck out her tongue at the three newcomers, waggling her fingers beside her ears.

"Nyah! A proper roast for a ghost!

Just wait'll I make a rhyme out of you.

Then you'll be proper citizens true!"

"Ahem," coughed O.Z. Diggs, regaining the populace's attention. "There is an extenuating circumstance that you may be interested in learning, I'm sure." He turned to Glinda, hoping the southern sorceress would better explain.

"Har har har!" interrupted the portly Red Jinn of Ev, elbowing the tall, lanky green sorcerer next to him. "Let's hear this, eh Zim? Of course you get *all* the credit, don't ya, Ozzy?" He laughed, rattling the lid perched atop his head so much that he had to snatch it off.

Zim, the flying sorcerer of Oz, merely raised an eyebrow in bemusement, and nodded. "We do best allowing the theatrics to be performed by the professionals," he mentioned.

The Wizard of Oz, at Glinda's urging and ignoring the taunt of his rival and the botanist next to him, spoke. "With the aid of our very *esteemed* friends, the Red Jinn of Ev and Zim the Flying Sorcerer, Glinda and I have succeeded in our task. It was no small feat, and—alas— Terrence, Christian, and... er, Klaus—though living, breathing new citizens of our lovely land of Oz—are basically... *ghosts!*"

A gasp of surprise passed among the celebrities gathered at the banquet.

Terrence rose. "We are grateful to your Wizards and the great Sorceress for restoring as much of our true forms as they possibly could." He leaned forward and kissed Glinda's hand graciously. The former prince stood before the Wizard of Oz and shook his hand, then did the same with the short Wizard of Ev, and the tall Wizard of the Seven Blue Mountains.

"You see," continued Glinda, "we were unable to restore them *completely*. Klaus' spell used a magic unfamiliar—and now lost—to us. They are substantial enough to be seen, heard, and felt, but they are nevertheless not completely whole."

As a demonstration, Christian stood and walked forward, his lower body passing through the table, amid more astonished gasps and murmurs.

In his own turn, Zim Greenleaf arose and addressed Ozma and her friends. "It was your gregarious pothos plant," he explained to the little queen, "that gave us the properties we needed. The plant's tenacious ability to grow and expand, whether nourished or not, is what I was able to harness and add to the spell." He nodded his head and bowed, his green plume of hair swaying like the leaves of a plant.

"I suppose they'll just have to be light eaters then," laughed the Red Jinn of Ev, amused at the reactions his joke received. "Har, har har! Get it? *Light eaters?* Ha! And if they stick around here, they'll *haunt* your palace! Your castle will be *haunted!* Har har!"

"Thank you, Jinnicky. I am so thankful that you were able to answer my call for help," spoke Ozma graciously. Turning to the guests, she added, "You are welcome to haunt this castle, if that is what you should choose."

"A toast, then," announced Terrence, raising a goblet of Ozade high in the air, "to the Haunted Castle of Oz!"

End of Part 1

Part 2
Chapter 1
Of Concern to the Queen

TWO years had passed, and Ozma was once again unsettled. What she had hoped to be a happy resolution appeared to be crumbling over time.

For the most part, Terrence, Christian, and Klaus appeared happy. They smiled and interacted with the other denizens of the palace. Christian, in fact, adapted best and even ventured out in the Emerald City with Button Bright and the other children. But the two men lingered inside, preferring to keep to themselves, and only on occasion, the company of Glinda, Oscar Diggs, and Ozma's closest friends.

The only problem seemed to be that Dorothy, Betsy, and Trot did their best to avoid them. Ozma knew full well of the frightening experiences they had encountered in Flora, but it disappointed her greatly that her dearest friends would be intentionally disdainful of them.

Zim Greenleaf, the celebrated flying sorcerer of Oz, had done the most traveling of all her subjects to other lands and dimensions. He was also most effective in creating peace and restoring health and healthy relationships. With a smile, Ozma realized just how blessed she was to have such a distinguished personage in her land. He and his wife Maggie were currently in the Emerald City, and the sound of his harp playing wafted up from the gardens to her in the throne room.

As so often they did, the Cowardly Lion and the Hungry Tiger napped on either side of her throne. She had concluded the day's business, entertaining visiting dignitaries, settling what few—and often rather silly—disputes that had arisen, and conferring with Jellia and other palace staff on the day's meals. Thankfully, the Hoppers and the Horners had not come into disagreement in quite some time. It appeared that there might be hope for lasting peace among those two squabbling peoples.

Ozma took mental stock of who she knew was currently present in the Emerald City, and could be easily summoned. There were Zim and Maggie entertaining in the garden. The three "ghosts" were present. Dorothy, Trot, Betsy and Button Bright lived in the palace, though Dorothy was spending time with her aunt and uncle on their farm on the outskirts of the city. Scraps lived in the palace as well. Polychrome had departed two weeks previously, when a rainshower brought with it a rainbow to aid her departure.

Ozma pulled a cord that rang a bell elsewhere in the palace. She waited in silence for Jellia to appear, holding her hands in her lap and smiling pleasantly. The two great cats that dozed beside her throne smelled of dandelions and fields. Gently, she stroked her hand across the purple stripe that ran down the Tiger's back, a reminder that he was a Gillikin animal. The Tiger stretched his hind legs out and front legs before him, licked his lips and turned to face Ozma. He smiled, yawned, and lay his head back down to continue napping.

After fifteen minutes had gone by, Ozma pursed her lips and looked about the throne room. Nothing stirred. The pothos plant was spreading along several hooks that had been placed in the ceiling, creating a draping canopy of vines and leaves. Zim had given the plant some special fertilizer, and the tendrils were spreading like mad. Soon they would have to install more hooks. Ozma made a mental note to ask Jellia to take care of that.

"Well, where are you?" she asked aloud, after twenty minutes had passed. Ozma arose from her throne and walked about the throne room. Her movement was enough to wake both the Lion and the Tiger. They arose and began pacing after her.

"What's the matter?" yawned the Lion. "Is there something going on?"

Ozma realized just how boring life as Queen had become. When her most exciting task each day was picking out the meals, surely something was amiss. "No, no," she demurred. "There is nothing wrong. In fact, most everything is *right*. We are... peaceful." She frowned, crossing her arms over her chest. "Everything is just peaceful."

She smiled at the Lion and the Tiger, patting them both tenderly on their heads. She addressed the Tiger. "Would you mind seeing if Prince Corum and Princess Marygolden have departed yet? If they are still here, I should very much like to speak with them again."

"Certainly!" agreed the Tiger, and he bounded off.

Turning to the Lion, she said, "I have a very special task for you, my friend; you and the Tiger, once he returns. But for now, can you find Benny the statue? And Kabumpo, too. I know I heard him this morning, so he and Pompa and Peg are probably visiting."

"Oh, they are all in the garden," replied the Lion, chuckling. "At Zim and Maggie's concert. Everyone's there, Ozma. Goodness. Why aren't *you*?"

Ozma blinked. "Indeed? Why am I not?" She smiled and took off running for the throne room doors. "Come on! Let's go to the concert!"

The lion bounded after Ozma and the two sailed through the corridors leading from the throne room out to the palace gardens. A grand crowd had gathered among

the flowering plants and trees. People from all walks of life mingled with each other; celebrities from the palace, vendors from far off lands, citizens, farmers, royalty and more were seated on benches or the grass as Zim and Maggie Greenleaf performed a gorgeous piece of music on the harp and theremin. The tall, green sorcerer deftly applied his hands to the dulcet strings of the instrument, plucking and gently coaxing out the gentlest of melodies, while the witch Maggie applied her own hands over the small, colorful box, waving them in motion to make an ethereal sound that accompanied her husband's playing.

Ozma recognized the tune as one he had played before: "Emotion in Motion." It was a song from the great outside world that the sorcerer had arranged to play on the harp. Hearing Maggie's theremin accompaniment made the tune even more lovely and otherworldly.

As the crowd realized who was making her way through, they graciously allowed her to come closer to the performers. The Wogglebug arose, and she accepted his seat on a bench next to Jack Pumpkinhead, who was holding his head with both hands, swaying in motion to the music.

"It's not an order, you know," she said to him. She then realized that Jack did not know the name of the tune; rather, he was swaying in enjoyment. "Oh. Nevermind, Jack dear," she added, when he swiveled his great carved head to regard her.

"Okay, Father," he said quietly, returning his attention to the concert.

Ozma took mental stock of the audience. There was Jellia, enjoying the concert. The Cowardly Lion had settled next to Dorothy and the Scarecrow, seated off to the side.

The girl ruler wrinkled her forehead in confusion. She had thought for certain that Dorothy was visiting her aunt and uncle on their farm. Shaking her head slightly, she continued to look around.

Notta Bit More, the circus clown, and his assistant Bob Up were seated nearby, as were Trot and Betsy. Standing or milling about were Scraps, the Frogman, Handy Mandy, Randy and Anetty of Regalia, and no one could miss Kabumpo. Ojo and his parents were among the visiting Munchkin dignitaries, and Nunkie was with them as well. Joe King and Queen Hyacinth were seated on another bench. Billina and some of her chicks were roosting underneath a juvenile lunch pail tree.

Notta certainly was resourceful. He would not be the first person Ozma would think of as tough, but definitely smart and quick to come up with plans. Handy Mandy lived up to her name. The girl had seven arms. Some of them were hard enough to be weapons themselves.

A handsome man sat with his wife and daughter across from her, and they waved. It took Ozma a moment to recognize Nick and Nimmee Chopper, with their daughter Forever Chopper. Standing behind them was a man in military regalia, who nodded politely to her. That would be Captain Fyter, in his flesh form. Ozma realized that Nick and Fyter had chosen to appear in human form, rather than in their tin bodies, in appreciation of all that Zim had done for them. "Captain Fyter!" muttered Ozma. "Yes, he'd be perfect!"

In another direction, she saw that the Hungry Tiger was successful in locating Prince Corum and Princess Marygolden. Making eye contact with the couple, Ozma gladly waved them to come sit with her and Jack.

Benny the Public Benefactor was standing stock still in the crowd, appearing to be the actual statue that he was. And there, next to him, stood General Jinjur! Perfect!

A young man in a striped, purple, tall hat stepped jovially around the crowd, dancing a waltz with another young man. They both wore brilliant smiles on their faces. Ozma recognized the fellow in the hat as Tommy Kwikstep, and the other as Perry, one of Jinjur's children.

With a smile, Ozma nodded. She would assemble a team—if they agreed to it—that consisted of Zim, Prince Corum, Captain Fyter, Notta Bit More, Handy Mandy, Benny, Jinjur, Tommy, Perry, the Lion and the Tiger. She shook her head sadly when she gazed at Kabumpo. The Elegant Elephant was most definitely one of the toughest individuals she had ever known. But he was also most definitely too big. And loud.

As Corum and Marygolden joined her, Ozma returned her attention to Zim and Maggie. She applauded with everyone else as they finished the tune, then congratulated the two magicians as they apparently had finished their concert. Ozma was quite glad to have at least been in attendance for the last song.

As the crowd began to disperse, Ozma asked Corum and Marygolden to remain, and managed to communicate to Tommy that she hoped to speak with Fyter, Mandy, Notta, and Benny, as well as with his partner, Perry, and his mother, Jinjur. The great cats remained with Ozma, and soon the audience consisted only of eleven people aside from her.

Zim, who was standing now with Maggie, bowed regally to the queen and spoke. "How may we be of service to you, Your Majesty?" he asked. The always-dapper sorcerer was dressed in a green silk shirt with dark green knee-breeches, and rich forest-green shoes with bright gold buckles. His wife, Maggie, wore a pink outfit with a billowing pink skirt and a magenta peaked hat. Her long, silver hair was tied back in a ponytail. Ozma still marveled happily at their disregard for each other's appearance. Zim, for all purposes, looked to be a young man in his 30s, while Maggie appeared to be an old dame in her 80s.

She regarded Tommy and Perry as well, smiling at the joy that the couple shared in each other. They sat together, holding hands and smiling genially back at the queen.

"I will be brief," spoke Ozma, gazing meaningfully and lovingly at each personage gathered in the gardens. "You may or may not know that we have three 'ghosts' living in the palace. Sir Terrence, Christian, and Klaus came here as refugees from another world. They escaped a kingdom called Flora, and from what I have been informed, it is indeed a dark, evil place.

"Yet the three of them are still not happy here. I had thought that granting them citizenship in Oz would solve their problems. Perhaps it has only..." she bowed her head, looking for the right words. "Perhaps that was only a temporary solution. Masking the problem, rather than confronting it and properly dealing with it."

"Excuse me, Majesty," interrupted Notta Bit More. The clown had been fidgeting as he sat, and now jumped up to stand before her, trembling. "You see, I... well, I don't really think... that is..."

Ozma held up her hand and addressed the clown. "I know that you are reticent to... to approach this subject. But they are *not* ghosts. They are merely different. And you must certainly agree that nearly everyone here is different in some way or another." She glanced meaningfully at Benny, Handy Mandy, the great cats, and the musical magicians. She swallowed and spoke again. "I certainly hope—and *know*—that there is no prejudice in this great land." Closing her eyes, she thought with chagrin about Dorothy, Betsy and Trot, and that the girls would soon come around to associating with the new citizens.

Notta's painted-on smile fell as his real face did, and he slumped his shoulders. Hanging his head in shame, the clown replied, "You're so right. I'm... I'm sorry." He raised his head and met her gaze. "Even if they *were* ghosts, that'd be no reason for me to... to... well..."

"Your point is made," said Ozma gently. Addressing the others, she turned slowly as she spoke. "Terrence, Christian, and Klaus are suffering. It is not their existence that is in peril. They exist here, and live here. They eat, sleep, and can do everything... well, *most* everything that flesh people can do."

"Begging your pardon," spoke up Handy Mandy, holding out three of her hands. "But what can *we* do to help them?" She looked about at the others gathered in the garden. "Looks to me like you've assembled a small army here."

At the word "army" both General Jinjur and Captain Fyter snapped to attention, their stern gazes looking to Ozma.

"Is there a reason why you've picked out those of us who appear to be more capably armed than others?" Handy Mandy looked a question at her queen, placing two of her hands on her hips. "I see that Omby Amby is *not* here, nor is Kabumpo."

"Those of us here," spoke up Corum, though looking somewhat quizzically at Notta, "appear to be more militant, or what you might consider as strong." He placed his arm around Marygolden's shoulders. "And I can presume that my wife is here as a courtesy to me, so that she is not left wondering what is going on."

Ozma blinked in astonishment as the conversation carried over on the tongues of the very people she was hoping to convince. She remained silent, waiting for them to speak their peace.

General Jinjur nodded, assessing the people gathered in the garden. "Mandy is, as she spoke, quite armed. I have taught my son how to handle weapons." She raised an eyebrow in defiance of Ozma's suddenly-shot look of disapproval and concern. "And Prince Corum is no stranger to wielding a sword. The good captain is exceptional with a bayonet." She nodded in approval as the fleshly form of Captain Fyter blurred and dissolved, reappearing in a shimmer as his metal form, the Tin Soldier of Oz. "Benny is a living statue, impervious to any attack, unless it be something gargantuan." The general looked at Notta through narrowed eyes. "The clown is a very smart man, and a very bad comedian. He is not as funny as he thinks he is. But he is quite clever, conniving, and even devious. I would rather have him on my team than opposing me."

Notta shrugged his shoulders, his eyes wide. He did not know whether to feel insulted or complimented. He tilted his head at the queen.

"Tommy Kwikstep has worked as a messenger. Since his extra appendages had been removed, he has become an even faster runner than anyone could have imagined;

faster than even the swiftest sprinter of Runnymede. I have personally witnessed his ability." She nodded approvingly at her son's partner.

"Do not underestimate us," growled the Hungry Tiger. His voice emanated from the depths of his chest, and shook the leaves on the plants around them.

"Of course," agreed Jinjur, nodding at him and the Lion. "You two are fierce, with brute strength. You may call yourself a coward, but you are indeed one of the bravest creatures I have ever come across." She pointed accusingly at the Lion. "Whatever Ozma is calling us to do will certainly need all the courage we can muster."

Maggie the witch clasped her hands in front of her chest. "My husband is no stranger to adversity. He has confronted fell beings and awful creatures that would make your hair stand on end. I would dare say that he is probably the strongest wizard in this land."

Ozma waited for the others to continue, but when it became apparent that they looked once again to her, she continued.

"You are all very astute. Thank you for giving me the time to speak with you. I shall come to the point. I want each of you to join me on an excursion to Flora. I want to go there with Terrence and his friends to see if we can help."

"And for that, you need an army of people to go along." Tommy Kwikstep stood up, letting go of Perry's hand. "This is going to be dangerous, isn't it?"

All eyes turned to face Ozma, and the queen felt the need to sit underneath that heavy gaze. Zim, seeing her need, offered the chair he sat upon during his performance to her.

All the while, Benny the Public Benefactor remained silent. Ozma looked to him first, feeling the stone man's coolness. With only the slightest movement, Benny nodded his chin downward, then upward again, and raised his arm to point at Tommy. Ozma understood, and answered his question.

"From what Dorothy, Trot, Betsy, and Button Bright told me, and from the reports that I got from Terrence, Christian and Klaus, the situation is dire indeed. We would be dealing with—*if* you accompany me—situations that none of us are accustomed to. It's... terrible. But I want... I *need* to do something about this. I have taken the three of them into our kingdom, but they are unhappy here. If they cannot be happy here, then the problem they were dealing with has not been solved; rather, it has only been avoided."

"*You* are going?" General Jinjur spoke. She wanted to make sure that she heard aright. Ozma nodded. "For this, you need people with you that can be counted on to function in dire circumstances." She stood from her seat and walked up to the queen seated upon Zim's chair. She knelt in front of her, bowed, then stood next to Ozma, laying a hand upon the queen's shoulder. "I stand with you, my queen! Far too long have we sat in complacency, living off the fat of the land! Such an opportunity does not often come along!"

Following suit, Captain Fyter, already standing, strode over to kneel before Ozma, then stand to her other side. The Lion and Tiger bounded up to kneel before her, purring their assent.

Zim gazed into Maggie's eyes as they stood behind the queen. The married couple did not need words to communicate. After only a moment's silence, Zim nodded and Maggie smiled encouragingly at him. "I will join you, my queen. Certainly a kingdom named Flora should have some interesting plants that I might sample."

General Jinjur glared sternly at her son, but Perry only fidgeted on the bench, clasping Tommy's hand in his own.

Making up her mind to join them, Handy Mandy also knelt before Ozma and pledged her fealty to the quest. That left only Corum, Benny, Notta, Tommy and Perry.

"Go," spoke Marygolden softly to her husband. She placed her hand on his back and pushed him forward to stand. "I will wait for your return. You need this." The princess wore a shoulderless gown and a tall hennin upon her head, all the color of gold. Her blonde hair hung in ringlets to the sides, and she brushed away a stray tear from her eyes. "Nay, 'tis only the wind that makes my eyes sting," she said to him. She waved dismissively at him. "Do go already."

The former Sir Hokus of Pokes, Prince Corum took a knee before the queen and spoke clearly to her. "I pledge my arm and my sword to thee, my liege and friend."

"Well, I suppose I'd better make up for the last time," laughed Notta Bit More, shoving his hands into his pockets and dancing about the bench he had been sitting upon. He strode forward and nodded to Ozma, though not effecting a full bow. "I'll help. Glad to be of service. Thanks for asking me." He smiled genially and turned to regard Benny, Perry and Tommy.

"There is no shame in refusing," spoke Ozma. "There are certainly more than enough willing to go with me." She arose from the chair and held the Tin Soldier's hand on one side and Jinjur's hand on the other. She smiled sweetly. "It's all right."

Perry cast an apologetic look at his mother. "I'm sorry," he said in a small voice. Jinjur gestured with her head that they depart, and Perry was happy to take Tommy's hand in his and leave.

Wordless, Benny strode forward and knelt before the queen. His leg and feet pressed down on the grass, leaving deep grooves in the lawn. Ozma nodded at the stone man.

"And so it begins," she breathed, looking up at the haunted castle of Oz. "Let's find our 'ghosts,' shall we?"

Part 2
Chapter 2
The Council is Convened

OZMA and her impromptu army adjourned from the garden to her council room. Jellia Jamb was summoned, and this time she was not distracted by a concert. The little queen requested that Jellia bring several trays of sandwiches and beverages to the council chamber, and to accommodate Maggie and Marygolden with suites in the palace. "Please have the Wizard join us," she requested. "And if Glinda is here, her too."

"Glinda has returned to her palace," explained Jellia as she gazed wide-eyed at the assemblage. She nodded to Maggie and Marygolden. "I will have rooms made ready for you."

"Oh, don't you worry about me, dearie," laughed old witch Maggie. She walked arm-in-arm with her husband to the council chamber with the others.

"I will be returning to our kingdoms," said Marygolden blithely as she walked with her husband. "There are matters to attend to. I trust my husband will return in due time."

"Please find Terrence and Klaus," the girl ruler said, "and if Christian is with them, him too." Jellia curtseyed and dashed off to the kitchens to make the preparations Ozma requested.

As an entourage, they struck quite an imposing presence walking the halls of the Emerald City palace, and those they encountered in the castle stepped aside in awe to see such a formidable group.

Led by the queen were Captain Fyter in his tin soldier form, with General Jinjur marching smartly next to him. Zim and Maggie Greenleaf followed, along with Prince Corum and Princess Marygolden, Notta Bit More the circus clown, the Cowardly Lion and Hungry Tiger, Benny the statue, and Mandy the goat girl from Mount Mern.

As they proceeded, Ozma searched her memory to determine if there were any other stalwart individuals that she could call upon to join them in their expedition. Tik-Tok came to mind, as did Nick Chopper. She dismissed Nick, knowing that the Tin Woodman had planned a special vacation getaway for his small family. She did not want to disrupt such a happy occasion.

That thought led her to further ponder disrupting the lives of the others already involved. Just how ethical was it to bring people into a potentially dangerous situation when their lives were perfectly wonderful? But that was just it—what point is there to living a wonderful life when confronted with the knowledge that others are not? Could living a wonderful life justify one from ignoring the sufferings of others?

She pondered, as they walked, whether or not to ask each of them—once more—if they were certain that they were willing to join her. Did they have any idea at all what sort of situation they were getting themselves into? In fact, did she? Only the "ghosts" could truly answer that. This situation was dangerous; moreso than she had previously thought. For all she knew, Ozma could be leading people to their deaths. And all for the happiness of three people that she had granted asylum to. How ethical was that?

Before any of them knew it, they had arrived at the council chamber. Twelve personages entered, including Maggie and Marygolden. There was no sense in sending off the wives. In fact, Ozma was hoping that Maggie might consider joining them on the expedition. They all sat at a grand, circular table, and Ozma could not help but smile at the notion that these were the knights of *her* "Round Table." Works of literature from the great outside world were quite familiar in Oz, and indeed, were great favorites among Ozma's people.

The kingdom of Flora was in another dimension. She, Glinda, Zim, Jinnicky, and the Wizard had determined that back when the refugees first were brought to Oz. Flora was not on Tarara either, of that she was certain enough. Captain Salt worked with Sheik Tazander of Ot'Sama to create a detailed map of the far off continent. Flora was not in any country of the great outside world, and thus it could only be deduced that it belonged to another realm of Faerie apart from the sphere in which Oz and An existed.

So, if Flora existed in a different fairyland, did the laws of magic and science work the same there? Ozma recalled Terrence's speech patterns. He spoke the same language she did, but under the enchantment of Oz, so did everyone. There was no foreign language except for those few that certain inhabitants chose to keep extant. The Wizard and

Dorothy spoke English, having come from America. But Terrence and his friends used words like "thee" and "thy" mingled with common forms of language. Were those archaic words from their own language, or something that the linguistic enchantment of Oz translated into rough equivalents?

Ozma realized that the children and the "ghosts" understood each other when they were in Flora; thus, she determined that their native language was indeed English. But as English was a language spoken in Great Britain, the United States, and other countries of the great outside world, it could only mean that Flora was, like Oz, connected to the outside world, and perhaps even once a part of it.

All of these thoughts weighed heavily upon the little queen, and as Jellia entered with three other palace servants bearing trays of food and drink, she placed her elbows on the table and rested her chin upon her hands.

Ozma was pleased to see Terrence, Christian, and Klaus enter the council room, and that they too partook of the sandwiches and drinks. In the course of the two years that they had been in Oz, all three were still exuberant about the variety and taste of the meals here. She wondered, then, if sending them back to Flora was justifiable after so long, but shook her head. The matter of tasty meals was not at stake here.

As the sandwiches were finished and people began looking to her, Ozma composed herself and arose to speak. However, before she could begin, the council door was opened. Perry and Tommy Kwikstep entered, followed by Tik-Tok and Jo Files. Ozma peered beyond them into the hallway, where Jellia Jamb waved and smiled quietly back.

Ozma returned the smile, glad to know that Jellia was so intuitive.

Perry and Tommy took two seats at the table, as did Jo Files, while Tik-Tok remained standing, his gears whirring and clicking quietly. General Jinjur narrowed her eyes at her son, but nodded in approval.

"I am grateful that you are all here," spoke the girl ruler to the large group of people assembled before her. She placed her hands on the table and leaned upon them. "What I ask of you is no small task." A click and movement behind her notified her that Oscar Diggs had entered the council chamber from a side door, and had quietly stepped up to join her.

Ozma resumed. "We are all gathered to..." She faltered, seeking the right words. Normally she would have practiced her speech, or at least thought about the topic before speaking; however, this council was quite impromptu. Thus, she hesitated.

"This is a council of battle," spoke up Jinjur as she folded her hands upon the table. "We are all gathered to sort out the issues with our guests' homeland, and attempt to overcome evil with good." She raised an eyebrow at Ozma. "Correct?"

"I stand in ser-vice e-ter-nal-ly to my com-mand-er, Oz-ma," spoke Tik-Tok mechanically. She was relieved to hear his words, but saddened nonetheless. As a mechanical man, he had no regard for his own self-preservation; only to serve as was his function.

"I want you all to consider what I am asking of you," she said. "You all have your own personal lives. You have happiness here in Oz, where we know—beyond a shadow of a doubt—that good will always overcome evil, and that evil cannot exist for long here.

"Two years ago we welcomed three people into our land from a kingdom called Flora, in another realm. That kingdom does not have the same enchantment that we do. People grow old and die there. Pain, misery, malice and pure evil exist there. Darkness exists there. But light exists too." She held up her hand toward the three "ghosts," who looked down uncomfortably. Klaus, especially, seemed disturbed at being thought of as anything like good. He suppressed a sneer and looked downward

"I had thought that you three would find happiness here. Perhaps you still can. But I see your sadness. I know what you have lost, and how you have sacrificed everything. Your home is not here, though I wish it would be." She lowered her gaze to the table, then looked up at them. "I would like to help you return to your home, if that is indeed what you desire. Tell me. Tell *us*. Is that what you desire?"

Terrence stepped forward, executing a bow. "Your Majesty," he said. "I fear my pain is rooted deep in my heart. I... *we* have lost much. Our families, our friends, pets, belongings, everything we had grown accustomed to all our lives."

Frowning, Klaus gazed downward and shook his head. "*Thy* lives, perhaps," he commented cryptically.

"The truth is, we would like to be happy here. We truly would."

"But we cannot," sighed Christian, looking up at the ceiling. "We left people behind we care about. My... my parents are there, somewhere. My sister, too. At least, I hope that they are."

Jaws dropped at this revelation. Handy Mandy placed

all seven of her hands over her mouth, and Ozma could only stare incredulously. Marygolden looked as if she might cry, but it was Maggie who arose and stepped forward to the ghostly boy. She smiled welcomingly.

Without speaking, the elderly woman held out her arms to him and embraced him as gently as possible, controlling her arms so that instead of passing through him, she instead spread warmth and comfort to him.

For the first time in ages, Christian allowed himself to let loose his fear and frustrations. The boy broke down in Maggie's arms. Maggie allowed everyone in the council room to fade away, and focused only on him. She began singing quietly, consoling him and assuring him, but allowing him to melt into his sadness. "I'll help you," she whispered, running her wrinkled old fingers through the boy's ethereal hair.

"All this time..." began Ozma. "Why hadn't you said anything?" A tremendous lump was threatening to choke her throat, and she fought down her own emotions. She shook her head.

"You've done so much for us, Your Majesty," spoke up Terrence. He sat glumly, folding his arms over his chest. Rubbing the thumb of his right hand across his forehead, he sat up and continued. "How much *more* can we ask? You have saved us. You have brought us to your home and welcomed us. Surely, in time, our lives will be good here. People can grow accustomed to anything. It just takes time."

Fearful and worried glances passed around the room. Ozma had almost forgotten her earlier concerns, but Christian's revelation only served to stir her into action. "I will go to Flora, and I invite any and all of you to accompany me. Regardless of who comes or who stays, I *will* go."

"Far too long have we sat idly by and allowed evil to grow and consume people!" Her fist slamming to the table, General Jinjur arose and barked out her words. "We have heard what happened in Tarara, when the evil filth of the Phanfasms was allowed to fester and taint the land. We know how many times the Nome King tried to attack us, and failed. We know of the Mimics and their evil desires, and they exist unimpeded on our very own continent. How much longer will we be *re*active and not *pro*active?" A snarl of anger and revulsion smeared Jinjur's face, and she cast her eyes upon each person present. "I challenge you, and I call upon it as your duty to begin a new chapter in our lives. A chapter where we not just live together in harmony and peace. A chapter where we make the lives of others better by eradicating evil and its threat, wherever that may be! Who's with me?"

The general's speech aroused the spirits of all in attendance. Cheers of agreement went up, and people spoke amongst themselves.

"But," spoke up the calm voice of Zim once the reaction had settled. "Do we have that right?" He gazed steadily at them all. "Is the solution, then, to invade by force and change the way other cultures work? Or do we instead invite the downtrodden to relocate to our land? If that is the case, then there are hundreds of thousands—millions even, if you include those from the outside world—who would like the opportunity to be here instead of where they are currently."

Christian peeled himself away from Maggie and wiped his eyes. "I have to help my family," he sniffled sadly.

"Indubitably. And we will assist you with that. Have no fear, my boy." The tall sorcerer nodded assuringly at him. "But the questions I ask are bigger than this. Bigger than all of us. General Jinjur suggests a military attack and what amounts to the domination of others. This was something that Captain Salt and his crew encountered on their travels—claiming lands in the name of Oz and forcing them to be under the protectorate of Ozma. Many times, the island nations that the good captain encountered had never before heard of Oz, nor did they care to be claimed as colonies. This policy of colonialism was stopped once we realized how imperialist it really was. I am not one to argue the ideals of good conquering evil. No doubt, there is evil in the land of Flora, and we have allied ourselves with the forces of good from that land. But beyond that, who is to say what is good and what is not good in other places? Who is to say we have the right to force our way of life upon other cultures that are accustomed to something different?"

Ozma nodded. "You are right, Zim. That is a moral question that should be addressed. But this council has not been convened for that. At least, not yet. This council is to determine who will join me in going to Flora to confront the evil that has taken over there, and do what we can to help whatever good is left." She addressed the general. "Jinjur. To some degree you are right, and perhaps we have stood by too long while evil spreads. We are doing something about it, and that starts now."

Ozma let out a deep breath, thankful that no others among the council had spoken. She was not sure she could rein in the discussion if they did, or even if she had the right to.

"Terrence, Christian and Klaus are under my protection. Thus, I have no problem in helping them to further deal with their problem as it extends back to their homeland. Whether or not we have the right to impose our will upon other cultures is not in question right now, and should that become pertinent, I wish for you all to be among whatever council that gathers to decide it. For now, I want two things. First, I want Klaus, Christian and Terrence to inform us of all the dangers and issues that remain in Flora. Second, I want you all to look within your hearts and decide, once again, if you are certain that you wish to join me in this. Can we do that without any more interruptions?"

Other than the members of the council fidgeting in their chairs and Tik-Tok's mechanical whirring, there was silence. The dull sound of stone scraping against stone as Benny raised an arm to point at the three ghostly figures. "Proceed," spoke the statue, his stone eyes unblinking.

From his seat, Klaus was the first to speak.

In the two years that the refugees had been in Oz, never once had they changed outfits. They ate when they thought to, but in the course of weeks and months they discovered that they did not need to. Sleep, too, had dwindled from their lives, though they still partook of that habit in order to rest their minds. Still, as semi-solid apparitions, their entire beings had been altered.

Klaus wore the same billowing robes he had worn when they first came to Oz. Reaching into one of his sleeves, the former wizard withdrew a leather-bound journal that was wound several times over with twine.

"The name I went by in Flora was Necronimus. It literally meant 'animator of the dead' and that was my duty. I was hired to work for Gorsbenor at a time when Terrence's parents, King Roust and Queen Shayle, still walked among us. This was when your uncle went by the name Lon," he explained, glancing at the former prince. "Terrence was but a child then, and as prince, his and my paths had no reason to cross. Yet one day they did, and I found myself reminded of a time when I worked as a toymaker, entertaining children and healing the sick and injured.

"I worked for Gorsbenor because I felt the need to change my stars. I had grown complacent in my previous work as a healer. I felt under-appreciated, and in fact I felt used. So I began to dabble in dark arts, and soon found myself as the necromancer to a devious usurper of a throne. Meeting a child and his dog amidst the darkness of Castle Flora reminded me that there were some things still worth fighting for. Some good left that was still worth preserving."

The former Necronimus unwrapped his journal as he spoke. He wound the cord around the palm of one hand, then thumbed through it to open the first page. "My first day of employ earned me twenty gold pieces, a tower workshop with a room to live in, a bed to sleep upon, and food allocation from the castle kitchen. On that day I was able to successfully reanimate the corpse of a soldier that had been run through—that very day—at the orders of Lon Gorsbenor. According to my notes, the man was lifeless for six hours before I was able to raise him. His state was trance-like. Any traces of his personality had left him. He followed orders that were given to him. He was able to stand, lift a sword and swing it. He stopped when Gorsbenor ordered him to. Aside from the ability to move and follow simple commands, the man appeared to be in terrible pain, moaning and wailing as he moved about. Many times he would pause to feel at the gaping wound in his chest, and would need to be reminded of his orders. This was a problem that Gorsbenor tasked me to remedy."

Klaus related to the ever-horrified council his attempts and eventual success in creating an army of undead that were not only completely subservient to Gorsbenor, but also not distracted by the fact that they were dead. The former wizard had concise notes relating to each day of his employment for the first few months. The notes then became sporadic; from weekly to monthly, and sometimes more in between.

Under Gorsbenor's direction, citizens of Flora were systematically arrested under false charges, or conscribed into the king's military. King Roust and Queen Shayle were quietly poisoned by Karloff and Pudgett.

Terrence gazed in growing horror and disgust at the man he thought was his friend. "You... you bastard," he uttered, pushing himself away from the table and rising. "You *knew*...?"

Ignoring Terrence, Klaus continued. "Due to the fact that I considered young Terrence and his parents *friends*, I daily counteracted the poisons with simple healing herbs and charms that I had brought over from my previous line of work. In direct violation of my employment with Lon Gorsbenor, I informed the king and queen of his subterfuge, presenting them with irrefutable evidence of his murderous intentions." He looked meaningfully at Terrence, who was still greatly troubled. "Under my direction, the king and queen elected to have their meals prepared by trusted family servants, the Monts." Klaus looked at Christian, who stood quickly up.

"That's my family!" said the ghostly boy. "My parents served the king and queen? Directly?"

"Indeed they did, my boy. You were but a child then, and you were charged with caring for your infant sister Jayne while your parents served the royal family."

Klaus glared at Terrence. "It was at my own peril that I turned on my employer. Your father, Roust, upon learning of his brother's betrayal, ordered his arrest and execution. I worked with him, unbeknownst to your uncle, to infiltrate his trust and subdue him. *I* worked with the *king*." He accentuated the first and last words, directing them hotly at Terrence. "Never once did I betray your family. Yes, I knew. But I acted on that knowledge."

"Please, Klaus," spoke Ozma softly, interrupting the discourse he was having with Terrence. "Continue your story. Terrence, I understand that you are upset. Let us hear him out. What became of the king and queen? And please let us know if there are any other dangers aside from the undead."

Klaus licked his lips and resumed.

"At the same time the King and I plotted to subdue his brother, Lon Gorsbenor sent his undead soldiers to dispatch the king and queen. We can only presume that he had grown tired of waiting for Karloff's poisoned food to be effective. It is also presumed that he allowed the young Terrence to live in order to give a modicum of legitimacy to his reign, as well as false hope to the people. The king and queen's demise was distressing, but it was blamed on a lingering sickness. The Monts were unwitting corroborators of that fable.

"Gorsbenor succeeded in murdering the king and

queen. My betrayal of him was not discovered, so I went back to work as the castle wizard under his rule. Gorsbenor ordered me to reanimate the bodies of the king and queen, but I cremated them instead, and animated two burned corpses in their place. Gorsbenor was none the wiser. I used my position to ensure the safety of young Sir Terrence. It was at that time that I became his tutor."

"What happened to my parents?" asked Christian. "The last time I saw them was... years ago."

Klaus turned to some pages in the back of his journal and read through them. "The Mont couple were arrested as conspirators against the prince regent, and sentenced to banishment. They were arrested, tried, and found guilty. Before their sentence was carried out, they were to be imprisoned in the castle dungeons until the next transport ship was scheduled to depart the harbor. I have no further record of their whereabouts."

"The dungeons were empty. They *have* been empty for years," spoke Christian darkly, looking at no one in particular. He slowly swiveled his head to regard Klaus. "And my sister?"

"I have no records of young Jayne Mont. It is my presumption that she has either been banished, escaped willingly, or may still reside in your family home in the hills of Flora."

"Two... two years... Why... why have you been silent so long?" asked Terrence, his voice cracking.

Ozma thought to interrupt the former knight's questioning, but thought better of it. She looked around at the other members of the council, and saw that they were all transfixed by the old man. Even Oscar Diggs remained silent. Apparently Tik-Tok's motion had wound down, though his thoughts still ticked away in his head. Ozma knew that someone would wind him up later.

Klaus looked at his friend and hung his head. "I was ashamed. I told myself that I was waiting for the right time to speak with you, but it was shame that kept me silent all these years."

"But... but you did the *right* thing," muttered Terrence, his own eyes soft with unshed tears. "You tried to help..."

"I *tried*." The old man nodded, then shook his head. "I tried, but I failed."

Silence followed. The Cowardly Lion shifted his weight and came to rest in a supine position. Benny's stone neck swiveled slightly as the statue turned from Klaus to regard Ozma once again. Deigning to break the silence, Jinjur placed one hand on the table and gently tapped at it with her fingernails.

"Is that it?" asked Mandy, drawing her seven hands away from her mouth.

Oscar Diggs cleared his throat and spoke up. "Ahem. You and the children had mentioned catacombs underneath the castle. You spoke of hearing... *sounds*... while you were escaping through the tunnels. What can you tell us about them?"

"Tell me this:" demanded Jinjur, interrupting the Wizard. "Do we go into battle?"

Klaus answered her simply. "Yes, we do. As for the catacombs: that is where the necromantic work was carried out. That is where you will find my failed attempts, and Gorsbenor's own experimentation. I would be of no use to him if he could manage the black arts on his own. Thankfully, if such things can be given thanks for, he was not successful. It takes innate magical ability to control any kind of magic."

Oscar Diggs nodded. He first worked in prestidigitation and as an illusionist, then learned real magic from Glinda and his own experimentation. He knew full well that his efforts would have proven fruitless had he not been born with magical ability.

"The catacombs are filled with failed experiments. But what is held in chains there may just prove to be more dangerous than the undead army Gorsbenor has control of."

"You didn't tell us any of this when we were in the tunnels," spoke up Terrence. "Why?"

"What sense is there in causing panic?" asked Klaus, addressing the other speaker. "The things I speak of are chained in the catacombs. We were not in any imminent danger as I led us out. Was that not so?"

Terrence remained silent. In his mind, he replayed the memory of their experience in the tunnel... the bloody handprints, and the fingernails caught in the walls. He bowed his head and pressed his lips together tightly.

"Where are the... *undead* soldiers kept?" asked Ozma. It was a challenge to wrap her mind around the word, much less force her lips and tongue to speak it. Seeing Jinjur's intake of breath and that the general would rise to interrupt again, Ozma raised her hand in her direction, indicating for the woman to stand down. "You will have an opportunity to speak in just a moment," she said to her. "I only want to know that answer right now."

"There is a sub-level in the castle," informed Klaus. He once again referred to his journal. Finding a page, he flattened the book and handed it to the girl ruler.

This was the first time that Ozma had actually handled

some of the ghostly substance that made up the three refugees. Their clothing and anything that they had upon their persons at the time of their exodus had converted to a semi-solid state. The book felt very light in her hands, and it was semi-transparent. Yet she could still hold it, and see upon its pages a detailed, side-view drawing of the castle, including the dungeons and catacombs.

"Turn the pages," directed the former necromancer.

Ozma did so, and saw even more detailed schematics. The following eleven pages each contained detailed maps. She looked up at him. "This is invaluable. Can I make copies of it?"

Klaus nodded. The little queen turned to Oscar Diggs and asked, "Do you have something that we can use to photograph this?"

"Your Majesty," spoke up Mandy. Up until this point she had remained silent. She spread all seven of her arms around herself, holding out her hands. She held out one hand to the book. "That is something I can easily do. May I?"

With a nod, Ozma handed the journal over to Mandy. From his little black bag, the Wizard of Oz removed a stack of paper and several pens and pencils. "Will this do?" he asked as he handed them over to the goat girl.

"Definitely," agreed Mandy, accepting the paper and the writing implements. "Watch."

Arraying six sheets of paper in front of her on the table, the multi-armed girl took six writing implements and began drawing, in unison, on each sheet.

General Jinjur arose from her seat and walked behind Mandy, observing with surprise how precisely the first map was copied simultaneously, six times over.

Perry joined his mother in watching the six hands draw while the seventh meticulously traced each detail, transferring the image from Mandy's fingertips to the other hands. Within moments, six exact copies of the castle schematic were being handed around the table, and Mandy began working on a second set of six. As she drew, she looked up. "One for each of us, right?" she mumbled, glancing quickly at the queen.

"Yes, oh do! Please!" Ozma allowed a smile to creep upon her face. She was grateful indeed that she had asked Handy Mandy to join her council.

Standing behind Mandy, General Jinjur spoke. "We will be seeing battle. That has been assured. To that end, we need to be equipped, armed and outfitted." She waved imperiously at Ozma, wrinkling her nose. "If you plan to lead this expedition, you cannot wear that dress or your crown. If we are to be in close-quarter combat, we need to be as agile and as slippery as possible."

"Slippery?" asked Notta Bit More.

"Slippery," echoed Jo Files. The soldier from Oogaboo stood up to address the council. "We need to give the enemy as few hand-holds as possible. That means long hair cut or tied up. Form-fitting, dense, durable clothes." He looked at the clown in his billowy outfit with brightly colored ruffles around his neck, hands and feet. "Nothing at all like that. Or that," he added, pointing to Tommy Kwikstep's peaked hat. "Or that," he continued, indicating Mandy's flared dress. The goat girl nodded, but continued to copy the maps from the journal.

Ozma agreed. She had read enough literature from the great outside world to know about military combat. She herself was no combatant, but she wanted to be equipped with protection, and did not want to be an easy target. It had been her policy, previously, to meet violence with non-violence. She recalled the defeat of the Phanfasms, Growleywogs, and Nomes as they tunneled up from below the Forbidden Fountain. It was a victory, to be sure, but it was temporary. Having drunk from the Water of Oblivion, the attackers lost their memories and were sent home. But soon those memories either returned, or were replaced with new directives similar to their initial directives. Sending them back to their people was a mistake. Ozma pondered many times over the years as to how she might have better done that.

"That is why I have gathered you," she said. "And I am grateful to you—Perry, Tommy, Tik-Tok, and Jo—for joining us. We need strength, cunning, and courage. We also need someone with the ability to heal, and..." She gazed at Zim and Maggie Greenleaf. "And, perhaps, someone who can possibly undo the evil that has been done."

"If I can remove the necromantic spell, I will," spoke up the tall, green sorcerer. "But if you are implying resurrecting the dead and giving them back their former lives, I've never done that before and I do not know about the ethics of such a thing. My heart tells me that even if it was possible, it would be wrong."

Ozma nodded. In her heart she knew such a request was impossible, but she wanted to explore every available option.

Steepling her hands before her, Ozma took a deep breath. "I need to know, right here and right now, from each of you: are you certain you are willing to join me on this quest? A simple yes or no will do."

"Yes," stated General Jinjur, as Ozma had expected.

"Yes," asserted Captain Fyter.

"Yes," whispered Zim, nodding politely.

"Yes," agreed Prince Corum, squeezing his wife's hand. Marygolden remained silent, knowing that the question was not addressed to her.

"Y-yes, I suppose," muttered Notta Bit More.

"Yes!" roared the Cowardly Lion, baring his teeth in a growl.

"Yes," echoed the Hungry Tiger.

"Yes," spoke Benny the statue, his gravelly voice scratching.

"Yes," said Handy Mandy almost dismissively as she continued to trace.

"Yes," Perry said, squeezing Tommy's hand below the table.

Tommy Kwikstep nodded in assent. "Yes," he said.

Tik-Tok's mechanical voice was the last to be heard. Blinking his metal eyes, the robot spoke. "Yes."

Part 2
Chapter 3
The Course is Laid Out

JENNY JUMP took some convincing. When Ozma and the war council came tramping into her Style Shop, the half-fairy girl was beside herself with ecstasy. The prospect of creating new outfits for Handy Mandy and Notta Bit More had intrigued her for quite some time, and it was highly disappointing to learn that they all needed to be outfitted with simple military uniforms.

Zim and Maggie both laughed. "You do realize, don't you," spoke Maggie to Jinjur, "that we are magicians, not soldiers. Besides, I seriously doubt we'll be engaging in hand-to-hand combat."

The first foray into outfitting the group was met with great disdain from General Jinjur, and though Ozma praised Jenny for the functionality and mobility of the uniforms, having them studded with emeralds and other gems was simply impractical. That, and as Jinjur pointed out, they would be walking targets in such garish outfits.

No, what was needed was simple grey bodysuits with simple clasps, pockets, and matching helmets. Ozma elected to go with United States Military Army helmets with kevlar and collapsible night vision goggles.

The proprietress of the Style Shop huffed and puffed, but begrudgingly adjusted the controls of her Magic Turn-Style to outfit the members of Ozma's council with military

uniforms to General Jinjur's and Jo Files' specifications. Captain Fyter and Tik-Tok needed nothing, as their metal bodies suited them fine for their duty. The same applied to Benny the statue. They all stepped through the Turn-Style and emerged in matching grey-green military fatigues.

There were grumbles from each of them as they regarded their uniforms, except from Handy Mandy, who was quite pleased with the utilitarianism of her seven-armed jacket.

"Let me give this a shot. I think I can find a happy compromise." She directed each of them—except for Mandy—to step through the Turn Style one more time. Jinjur took the lead, and emerged decked out in military dress blues. Corum, following, appeared in fatigues that were covered with sand-yellow and golden patches. Jo Files' old private's uniform, which he wore when Queen Ann set out to conquer Oz, appeared on him, restored and pressed. Notta Bit More, on the other hand, stepped through and emerged wearing an archaic French military uniform, with flared knickers and a disc helmet. Perry and Tommy stepped through with more stylish and modern uniforms with embroidered Oz insignias.

Jinjur blew out a breath, rolled her eyes, and relented. "That will do just fine. Thank you Jenny."

There was no point in tactical training. Ozma specifically hand-selected members of the council who she knew would be efficient in combat.

"I presume, Your Majesty," spoke Oscar Diggs to his friend as they adjourned for another day to the council chamber, "that you have a plan to transport this entire army to Flora?"

Ozma frowned. Her adamant insistence on helping Terrence and his friends had taken upon itself such momentum that the detail of transport had been overlooked.

Klaus' difficulty in successfully transporting himself, Christian and Terrence to Oz gave her pause. The wizard managed to transport the children back to their home, but he was merely returning them to their home dimension. The wizard's magic also managed to enable Terrence to bring the four of them to Flora in the first place. Somehow the back-and-forth of it did not make sense to anyone.

"I want you to speak with Klaus," she replied. "You and Zim. The Great Jinjin is visiting, so I want you to ask him to join you. The four of you should be able to figure something out. I want you to start with whatever spell Klaus used to send Terrence to Oz. Follow that with the spell he used to have Terrence bring Dorothy, Betsy, Trot and Button Bright to Flora, then whatever magic he used to send them, and himself, Christian, and Terrence back here." Ozma nodded as the Wizard of Oz hastily scratched notes on a notepad that he swiftly had extracted from a coat pocket.

"I'll find out if it's a temporal dislocation or displacement problem. If it's a matter of transmission—such as if his spell can receive completely, but transmit incompletely—that would explain why they came here as ghosts, but our people went there solid."

To the rest of the council, Ozma announced, "We should tentatively be ready to travel to Flora within one week's time. The more time we spend here, the more danger any survivors who remain there will be in. The Wizard, Zim, and Klaus will be conferring about the matter of transportation. If the great Tititi Hoochoo is available, I have asked that he be involved.

"Jenny Jump has kindly outfitted all of us who need it with uniforms and helmets. General Jinjur has been in contact with Queen Ann of Oogaboo, and we will be receiving a shipment of shields, swords, and spears." She felt the need to remind everyone in the council of her stance against violence, but that had been established. This was an abnormal situation; one that the little queen hoped would never again happen. If General Jinjur had her way, such forays would increase. She shook her head. Weapons and intentional invasion were the antithesis of everything she stood for. A tear welled up in her eye, but she blinked it away. The greater good was at stake here.

Ozma bit her lip, and continued to the next topic: delegation of responsibility, accountability, and leadership. She had considered appointing Jo Files over General Jinjur, but realized that such ranking would distress the general to such a degree that there would be no order. No, she knew that Jinjur needed to be in charge in order to keep the peace. Ozma almost chuckled at the thought of keeping peace in a council of war. Such concepts canceled each other out.

Thus, Ozma directed that Jinjur would be top ranking, answerable only to the little queen herself. Ozma, being a pacifist, informed them that her duties would include protection and rescue of innocents, as well as reconstruction and repair as needed. Under General Jinjur the next highest ranking members would be Jo Files and Perry. Notta Bit More was appointed as strategist, to work with Zim. All of the other members of the team were to work as offensive and defensive forces.

A battle was waging within Ozma. She recalled how she would rather have been overcome by the Phanfasms and Whimsies and Nomes, than raise a finger in violence. Spread before her on the council room table were maps of Castle Flora. Gathered around the table were some of the most physically powerful and militant people in her entire land.

Another sensation was stirring in the girl ruler's body. Her stomach was convulsing, and her head was pounding. The pressure behind her eyes was intense, and enough to make her see stars. She took a moment to recollect something that Dorothy had said to her only days before.

"Ozma, I have a headache."

Such a statement seemed so innocuous, but the more Ozma thought about it, the more she realized that such a thing could not occur in her land. She blinked, realizing that she, too, had a headache. And more than that, her stomach hurt. Her mouth was dry, and her vision was beginning to blur.

And then Ozma made another decision. She met eyes with Zim, who had been conferring with Notta and Maggie. The tall wizard knew that his queen needed to speak with him in private. He arose from his seat, excused himself, and followed Ozma to the back of the council chamber.

"I cannot do this," she said in a hushed whisper.

"I know, Ozma," spoke Zim. He placed his hand on her forehead, frowning. "This will not do." Turning to Maggie, he spoke. "Ozma has a fever. This is the third fever in the past week." He scrutinized the little queen. "You need to go to bed. Jellia has some medication that I've given her for the others. She will tend to you."

Ozma blinked in surprise. "Who... who are the others?" she asked. In her heart, she knew that they were either

Dorothy, Trot, Betsy, or Button Bright.

"Betsy Bobbin and Dorothy Gale. The herbs that I gave Jellia took care of their fevers within a day. I do not see that this is an issue. Tonight you sleep." The tall sorcerer placed Ozma's hand into his arm and allowed her to lean on him. They walked to the door of the council chamber, with Maggie on Ozma's other side. "Tomorrow, the Sawhorse will take you, Dorothy and Betsy to Glinda's palace. From there, three of you will be traveling with Glinda to Burzee. Oscar Diggs will take the Magic Belt and keep watch over the land while you are on sabbatical. This has all been arranged. Jellia Jamb will attend to you. So long as you are ill, you cannot afford to concern yourself any longer with what is going on behind these doors. As your friends and counselors we must absolve you of these matters."

And as simply as that, Ozma allowed herself to be escorted from the council chamber to the hallway, where Jellia anxiously awaited her. The little queen was nauseous and in shock, and could not believe that her friends and subjects would usurp her control. Was it the fever that made her think these thoughts? Or had she just started her kingdom down an elusive slippery slope? She spoke aloud her thoughts. "It was I who suggested helping Terrence's people, but... not like this, not without me there."

Zim only smiled and said, "The Jinjin has taken down the Magic Picture. But it is merely for a few hours. I trust he has good intentions. I believe he is fixing a scratch on the frame. There's no need for you to look into it before you depart for Glinda's palace. Oscar and the Scarecrow will check it regularly. You need to get well."

Ozma looked sternly at him. Her mouth was dry, and her heart threatened to beat out of her chest. "I will not condone violence," she breathed, her eyes almost melting the tall wizard.

Zim placed his hand on her shoulder, smiling assuredly at her. "I'm sure I don't know what you mean, Your Majesty." As the little queen began walking with Jellia, Zim stayed behind at the closed door to the council chamber. As an afterthought, he added, "No living beings will be hurt in anything I involve myself in. I promise you that."

Ozma turned to the tall wizard and nodded as he bowed deeply to her. "It had better not."

Part 2
Chapter 4
What Makes You Different?

NEXT MORNING found Ozma, Dorothy, and Betsy riding the Red Wagon behind the Sawhorse, south from the Emerald City. Button Bright and Trot elected to join them, and Ozma was glad for their company. However, more important to her was keeping all of them together. If they had contracted some foreign virus from Flora that caused whatever malady she had felt the night before, she did not want to expose anyone else to it. Being closest to all of them, she realized that she had the most exposure. However, there were hundreds of interactions among the denizens of the Emerald City, including Aunt Em and Uncle Henry.

Ozma frowned, acknowledging the slight headache that still lingered. She understood that Zim was sending them away not only to put distance between her and the unpleasant business they attended to, but also to work with Glinda, Zurline, Ak, and other powerful beings in Burzee to ensure that if a cure was needed, they would come up with it.

Her frown turned into a smile. Zim indeed was a wise wizard. Wise and intuitive. It was preemptive to travel to Burzee. In the off-chance that there was indeed something making them sick, its effects would be lessened and dealt with.

She smiled at the other children riding with her. "It's going to be a lovely day, today. Don't you think?"

"It's always a lovely day," sighed Button Bright, leaning back on the rear seat of the wagon and throwing his arms over the back.

"But that's a good thing," insisted Trot, smiling emphatically at Ozma. She knew that her friends had been feeling poorly, and wanted to bolster their spirits.

"Why have you been avoiding the 'ghosts'?" asked Ozma abruptly. She asked the question generally, not directing it at any of the children.

The silence that followed her question was almost deafening. Even the Sawhorse slowed down his usual trot to listen.

The little queen looked at each of her companions, smiling encouragingly. "You can tell me," she urged. "I understand that you encountered... rather, experienced, some terrible things with them. I don't mean to pressure you. You can certainly spend time with whomever you please. I just could not help but notice that you avoided them."

Button Bright, normally quiet, was the first to answer. Despite their appearance, all five of them were so much older than they looked. Though they remained childlike in many ways, with age comes wisdom. "The wounds are too fresh," he said, tilting his head slightly. He paused, thinking, then spoke again. "They're nice. I like Klaus a lot. But being with them..."

"Is strange," interrupted Trot, casting a glance downward at the wagon wheels as they turned. She looked up, placing her hands in her lap. "It's... not that we don't like them. Button Bright's right. They're nice. But... they just..."

"They don't belong," blurted out Dorothy suddenly. Her eyes agog, she clamped her hands over her mouth. She realized what she had spoken was completely against anything and everything she had ever known in Oz.

The words stung Ozma, as well as the others, including Dorothy herself. The little girl from Kansas held her face in her hands.

Once again, silence ensued, and the Sawhorse took this as his cue to pick up his pace.

Ozma wanted to ask Dorothy why she felt that Terrence, Christian and Klaus did not belong. She chose not to speak her question, and pondered it herself.

Jack Pumpkinhead was constructed to scare a witch. In fact, there were witches in Oz. Terrybubble was an animated dinosaur skeleton. The Scarecrow was possessed of the life-force of a dead emperor. But what made them so *not* scary? And what was it that made the refugees from Flora *so* scary? If one considered them "ghosts" then that was not enough. Their forms were semi-transparent, and they were partially intangible. That was not enough. What made them scary? And was the term "scary" the right word to use?

"Different" was not the right word either. Everything about everyone in Oz was different. The Frogman. The Patchwork Girl. The Tin Woodman. Tik-Tok. Zim. Handy

Mandy. Kabumpo. They and more were so wide and varied that being different was pretty much being normal.

All Ozma could consider was that Terrence, Christian and Klaus were a different kind of different. They kept to themselves, like the Lonesome Duck did. They were quiet, like Benny the Statue. They were sad, and morose... like... like no one else. But was being melancholy such a crime? Was that worthy of the stigma that made them so outcast?

Ozma resolved to have a serious talk with her friends and subjects once this was all taken care of. But then she realized that she was already having that serious talk, and that nothing had yet come of it. And the part about it being taken care of... that was a very unpleasant concept that the little queen did not want to think about.

Her headache had returned, and her stomach was cramping again. She steadied herself by holding onto the side of the wagon as she doubled over. Pale and sweating, Ozma saw that Dorothy, Betsy, and now Trot were all looking as queasy as she felt.

"Sawhorse," she said as her breathing quickened. "Hurry. Bring us to Glinda as fast as you can." She smiled as best as she could, hoping to reassure her friends. "I have some of the lozenges that Zim gave us to take along," she said as the wind began whipping at her hair. She retrieved some wrapped lozenges from the picnic basket that Jellia had sent with them. "Take one. Each of you. You too, Button Bright."

All five of them put the sorcerer's remedy into their mouths and let them dissolve on their tongues.

Ozma took Dorothy's hand in her own, and saw that each of them were holding onto each other. Whatever it was that had made them ill was recurrent. A cure needed to be found, and the best hope for that lay in Burzee. It was a relief to know that the most powerful of immortals would be able to help them.

The springs and joints on the Red Wagon were recently upgraded by Tik-Tok. Despite the high speed with which they traveled, and the occasional bumpy terrain, Ozma and her companions traveled in great comfort and ease.

Part 2
Chapter 5
The Day of the Departure

BATTLE was an unpleasant business. General Jinjur had experience with it, as did Tik-Tok, Captain Fyter, and Jo Files. Regardless, plans were made, weapons were divvied up amongst the combatants, and every imaginable scenario was discussed. Not since the debacle where a dictator from the great outside world had come to Oz had there been such an organized effort. True, their force was a tiny fraction of the force that had been gathered by that nefarious man; but what they lacked in volume they more than made up for with strength, ability, and determination.

Utilizing the former necromancer's journal and the combined skills of Tititi Hoochoo, Zim, Maggie, Oscar Diggs, Glinda, and Jinnicky, the magic-users felt confident that they could recreate the spell that would transport people from Oz to Flora as well as return them to Oz; however, transporting people from that dimension to Oz was still a grey area. Ozma's suggestion about transmission interference resonated with them all, and the great Jinjin agreed that dimensional portals were tricky to deal with. Even he could guarantee nothing when it came to trans-dimensional rift traveling.

Zim was the mastermind behind the return portal. In his travels, the flying sorcerer had picked up some good working knowledge of portals, and knew that their success depended on a way for them to get back home. Such a "back door" could not be left unattended or open, however. Thus, once he and the Jinjin perfected the spell to call the return portal open, Zim ensured that each member of the excursion had it memorized by rote. It was a simple matter of coming up with a rhyme that communicated the nexus of the spell. The ability to cast the spell depended on a combination of concentration and a certain charm. Wording it as a rhyme allowed the speaker to focus.

With Maggie, Zim meted out charms to each member of the team. To Tik-Tok's side, right underneath his arm, the sorcerer mounted a silver gear. He used droplets of liquid silver from a crucible that the metal man himself held. The white-hot metal solidified and permanently adhered the gear to his side.

To the Cowardly Lion and Hungry Tiger, Zim presented thick collars made of spun silver, gold, and steel. The material was surprisingly pliant, and did not cause the great cats any discomfort.

"I will need you to revert to your human form for this," instructed Zim to Captain Fyter, who complied readily. The human form of the Tin Soldier appeared where he stood.

"What now?" asked the man of flesh and bone. He twitched his shoulders and moved his head about.

Reverting to human form sometimes took him by surprise. He scratched his head.

"Hang this around your neck," instructed the sorcerer, handing him a toothbrush tied to a cord. Captain Fyter grasped it in his hands and looked at it.

"This is my own toothbrush," he said, looking at the sorcerer. "How did you get it?"

Zim shook his head. "Simple summoning spell. Put it around your neck and turn back to tin." He nodded as Captain Fyter did so, then continued with the others.

"Each of you must guard your charm. It is what will bring you back here. Each charm is either a personal effect of yours, or made from materials one can only find in Oz. Each charm has a strong magnetic and magical pull to our homeland." Zim nodded to Handy Mandy, who, like the others, was dressed in her military uniform fatigues. "This is your cap," he said, handing the white cloth headgear to her. "Keep it close to your heart."

To Prince Corum he handed a large red feather. "This was the plume worn upon your helmet when you were enchanted. Sir Hokus of Pokes is no more, but he is part of your history. Guard this well."

Corum raised his eyebrows and smiled, gladly accepting the feather. Its shaft was broken and bent in several places, but that did not matter to him. "Thank you, Sorcerer! I shall guard it well!"

Notta Bit More presented an interesting sight. The fellow insisted upon wearing his clown makeup, and over the years he had worked with the Wizard, Glinda, and local artisans to come up with makeup that was nearly permanent. It would be nigh impossible to remove the white-face, big red lips, and eye dots. Seeing a soldier with clown makeup might have appeared funny, but they were all accustomed to his appearance. With a smirk, Zim handed him a red rubber clown nose. "Keep this safe," he said to Notta, who promptly stuck it upon his real nose.

"Don't worry," assured the clown. "I'll tuck it away somewhere safe once we head out."

To Benny, Zim spoke next. "You presented a challenge to me, but I believe we can get you equipped." Zim turned to his wife, who had been helping him dole out the charms. She reached into his bottomless satchel and pulled out a grey belt. "This comes from our old ally, King Kaliko of the Nomes. It is woven from Ozian rocks. The Nomes work quickly. We were able to transport a wheelbarrow full of gravel to Ev, and within a day we were able to get this back. It's good to have friends."

"Thank you," muttered the statue, accepting the belt. He found it difficult to tie it about his waist, but Corum and Notta helped him to secure it.

"A feather?" asked Jo Files as he accepted the next charm.

"Not just any feather," said Zim with a smile. "Look closely at it."

"Oh! It's from another Benny! Benny the Gander," exulted the soldier from Oogaboo. "This is perfect!" Jo's friend was a Canadian goose named Benny, with whom he and his wife Ozga had experienced a most unusual adventure that involved an enchanted castle. Private Files smiled and tucked the feather inside his jacket.

Tommy Kwikstep was given a shoe buckle. "This is from a shoe that I retrieved from your home," explained Zim, handing an identical one to Perry. "As partners, I felt it was only fitting to give you both a matched pair." Both young men took the blue metal buckles and put them in their jacket pockets.

"Glinda, Oscar Diggs, the great Jinjin, Klaus and I are ready to initiate transportation." He glanced at the Wizard of Oz, who remained in attendance with the council. Diggs nodded. Zim then turned to General Jinjur. "Then, at this point, I move that we all direct our attention to General Jinjur. From this point onward, she is in charge. I expect we will all follow the good general's direction."

"Right then," spoke General Jinjur. She regarded the faces of all the members of the search and rescue task force. "I will treat you with the same amount of respect that you give me. We are a team first and foremost. I am in charge. If you have anything to discuss with me, I will hear you. When it comes to split second decisions, count on me. We will be successful." She allowed a smirk to creep upon her face, then barked out, "Attention!"

Private Files, Perry, and Captain Fyter snapped to stand and salute the general. Benny and Tik-Tok remained standing, and turned to face the general. The others looked at them in bewilderment, realizing that their first military order had been given. Mandy, Corum, Notta and the rest stood, straightened their shoulders, and looked at Jinjur for further instruction.

Nodding, Jinjur looked at each of them. She set her jaw, turned on a heel, and began marching around the table to the doorway.

"Fall in!" ordered Private Files, who marched smartly behind her. The clomping steps of Captain Fyter, Tik-Tok, Benny, and the remainder of the team filled the hallways of the Emerald City palace.

Word of the group meeting in the council chamber had spread among the castle denizens. As the sound of metal, stone, and boot-shot feet filled the palace, the hallways were vacated. Even the great throne room was emptied. As the team trooped into it, they were gladdened to see two lone figures waiting for them before Ozma's throne.

Prince Corum's charger, Stampedro, shifted his bulk as he waited for his master. Upon seeing the prince of Corumbia enter, the horse neighed and shook his mane happily.

The other figure arose from a seated position, spreading out a vast span of grey-feathered wings.

"And you are?" demanded General Jinjur, advancing upon the winged monkey that stood in their path. The doorway to the Wizard's secret chamber was behind the throne, and it was there that the other magicians awaited them.

"My name is Kak. I was visiting my friends Maybe the Miffin and Snif the Iffin, and they told me what was going on. I want to join you."

Kak was no longer the juvenile winged simian that Oz's griffins had encountered years before. The monkey was fully mature, and as Jinjur could see, well-muscled, agile, and with the ability to fly. Corum's horse was a knight's charger, and trained in battle. She turned to Zim. "They will need charms. We can teach them the words along the way." She paused a moment, then asked the tall wizard, "What is your charm?"

"We are each other's charms," answered Maggie the witch, speaking for her husband. General Jinjur noted, with some surprise, that Zim's elderly wife had changed from her normal frilly dress into some kind of ancient battle dress, possibly Median; it was a nice effort to match the rest of the team. Jinjur threw her head back as she scrutinized the witch. It suited her. "Very well then. What are the words?"

Maggie let go of Zim's hand and stood alert before the general.

"Our mission is true, victory is ours.
We shall not bend to any powers.
No more fighting, no more claws.
It's time to return, our home is Oz."

The little witch saluted smartly, clicked her booted heels together, and lowered her arms to her side.

General Jinjur turned to Stampedro and Kak. "You will be given charms. Guard them with your lives. Learn those words. That is your ticket home. Zim!" she barked, turning to the tall sorcerer. "Charms. I trust you have extras?"

"I do." Zim produced a gold ring from his satchel and gave it to Kak. "Wear this. Protect it. Touch it and recite the spell when you're ready to return here.

"You do not have grasping appendages," spoke the tall sorcerer to Stampedro. "This might prove difficult, but we were able to give a charm to Benny and to Tik-Tok, so I'm sure we have something that will work for you."

"You'll have to touch it and recite the spell," advised Maggie, rummaging around in the bottomless satchel. "Can you touch your snout to your chest?"

The horse nodded emphatically, arching his neck to demonstrate. "Easily," he said.

Maggie produced an old-fashioned key from the satchel, which Zim then fastened to Stampedro's reins. "This will have to work," sighed the sorcerer. "Mind you take care not to let anything happen to it." He addressed Corum. "This is your duty, as well. You and your steed will be as one unit."

"I'm glad Marygolden left for home. I fear whatever may transpire during this... tour of duty," said the yellow knight. He spoke to his horse. "And I'm glad you are coming with me. It will be just like old times."

"Somehow I doubt that," muttered the Cowardly Lion to the Hungry Tiger. Both of the great cats plodded along with the team as they marched behind Ozma's throne and into the Wizard's hidden chamber.

"I can't imagine their idea of old times involving what we are about to do," sighed the Hungry Tiger, licking his chops. He groaned. "It's ironic; for the first time I'll have the opportunity to devour another creature, but they're so... *ruined* that I don't dare!"

The Lion nodded his great head in agreement.

The team trooped into the Wizard's chamber and encountered him, along with the Red Jinn of Ev, the great Jinjin Tititi Hoochoo, Klaus, as well as a tall woman with long, flaxen hair and an ornate golden crown. Next to her stood a woman in a bright red dress with wavy, dark brown hair.

"We came as soon as we could," explained the witch from across the northern desert. Queen Zixi of Ix was holding a dried up twig in her hands, which Zim recognized to be *Acacia craspedocarpa*. This pleased him greatly, and he nodded to the witch queen.

Maëta of Mo stood next to Zixi, and nodded to the assembly. She too held a wand, though hers was polished and rigid.

"Elderberry?" the botanical wizard asked.

Maëtta looked at her wand, then nodded. "Red elderberry, yes."

"*Sambucus racemosa*. Excellent. We are glad to have you both with us," replied Zim, and stepped away from the gathered team to join the magic-users.

"This is a special circumstance, where I feel we could use the aid of one more magician," commented Oscar Diggs. His gaze passed over all the people and animals assembled in the room. "As acting ruler of the Emerald City in Ozma's absence, I propose that we all grant special dispensation to Klaus, former wizard of Flora, to make use of his innate magical abilities."

"For this one occasion only, I would amend," added Zim. "If he is agreeable to such terms?"

The former necromancer nodded, his mouth clamped shut in grim determination. Under Klaus' direction, the combined magical abilities of Zim, Oscar Diggs, Jinnicky,

Zixi, Maëtta, and Maggie conjoined.

"The doorway," directed Oscar Diggs, pointing to where the others had just entered. "We can use that for the portal."

Twenty heads turned to regard the door that they had all passed through at some point. The Wizard of Oz stepped through the crowd and approached the door. Retrieving his own wand from his coat pocket, he reached it out to touch the left side frame. Tracing upward with the wand, Oscar Diggs focused his energy through the wand and into the doorway. He reached upward, to the right, down the side, and across the bottom. As he returned the wand to the spot on the frame where he started, the little man spoke some words under his breath, sealed the spell, and stood back.

Maëtta, Zixi, Tititi Hoochoo, Zim and Maggie repeated his spell, and then Klaus tentatively approached the now-glowing frame. The ghostly wizard took a deep breath, then traced the shape of the door frame with his own outstretched hand. The same words spoken by the other magicians rolled off his tongue, and he stepped back. The doorway appeared unaltered, and they could see the throne room out beyond the opened door.

"Is that it?" demanded General Jinjur, striding angrily toward the door. "Why, this is noth—"

As Jinjur passed through, she abruptly disappeared.

"And that is how we shall do this," spoke Zim curtly. He took his wife's hand, and the two of them stepped forward. "We don't need to leave our commander alone in a foreign land. Come on!"

As the Greenleafs disappeared, the others gathered their wits and began following.

"Where will we end up?" asked Tommy Kwikstep of the assembled magicians.

"West courtyard of the castle," muttered Klaus darkly, watching as the team began to vanish through the doorway one by one. "It will be out in the open. Be prepared to defend yourselves!"

The Tin Soldier, Tik-Tok, Kak, Corum and Stampedro, Notta Bit More, Handy Mandy, and Private Files had already stepped through the portal, leaving only Tommy and Perry.

General Jinjur's son took a deep breath, swallowed, and stepped forward toward the door. Before passing through, he reached back to grasp Tommy's hand. "Let's do this," he said to his partner.

The young Gillikin man nodded, his eyes wide. The military helmet slid down over his right eye, and he reached up to push it clear of his vision. "A-all right," he faltered. "All right. Let's go!"

And they passed through the door.

"I'll be taking my leave, then," demurred Zixi, nodding to the others as the team of Ozians vanished. She looked askance at the wizard. "You will not be watching them in your search screen? I had heard of it. Certainly it can peer through dimensions...?"

Oscar shuddered, glancing at the assembled magicians. "That it did... er, does. But... something... it's not a one-way screen. That is to say, it... well, something looked back at me the last time I used it. I don't use it anymore."

Zixi and Maëtta both nodded, understanding. Klaus made a mental note of it.

Part 2
Chapter 6: Good Medicine

GLINDA welcomed her guests readily, having known about their arrival from the great Book of Records.

"Ozma, Dorothy, Button Bright, the Sawhorse, and Trot are on their way to visit Glinda with a virus."

As usual the book's message was cryptic. The concept of a virus was unheard of in Oz, but Glinda knew what it was. The Sawhorse was speedy, true, but Glinda had enough time to research the topic before they would arrive. Medical journals from the great outside world had found their way into Glinda's library, and she consulted as many of these as she could, endeavoring to understand what a virus was and how to deal with it.

An anti-virus seemed to be the only logical remedy, but that was often created from the virus itself. As antivirals were also found in the essential oils of certain herbs, an apothecary's knowledge was needed, and the best person for the job was Herby, the Medicine Man of Oz. According to the Book of Records, Herby was in the Ozure Isles, visiting Prince Philador. That made sense to her, but was inconvenient. Word was sent by the crow network to him. Glinda gave the crow a whistle to carry, with instructions that Herby should blow it three times to be transported to her palace.

Beyond that, Glinda could do nothing more than continue her research.

Once Ozma and her friends had arrived, the southern sorceress was pleased to see them in good spirits and relatively good health. Ozma exhibited signs of a headache, but the girl ruler quickly brushed off Glinda's concern. "Zim's lozenges will take care of it," she assured her old friend. Ozma made eye contact with Glinda, communicating her need to stay positive in front of her friends. Glinda could see that the fairy ruler of Oz was worried.

Nodding, Glinda said, "Good. I'm glad of that. Still, let's see if we can get all of you taken care of. The swan chariot will take us to Burzee in the morning. I have sent word for a friend to join us, if he is able."

Entertaining guests was something that Glinda was accustomed to, but in this instance all five of her guests declined the usual banquet that the southern sorceress suggested. Instead, Ozma suggested that they all retire to Glinda's own private apartments and have a quiet meal.

"I could sure enjoy some tea right now," requested Dorothy softly, grimacing slightly as she rubbed the sides of her head.

Glinda was expecting discomfort among her guests. She should have known better than to suggest a banquet.

She chided herself for the foolish choice, then focused on what she could do to make them comfortable.

The Sawhorse was loosed from the reins and allowed to wander off in Glinda's palace. The wooden steed ambled to an inner garden spot and contented himself with watching the grass grow. To his great delight, a ladybug was slowly crawling upon one of the blades of grass, and the Sawhorse felt he could be satisfied for hours watching it... and he did.

Trot, being physically the youngest of them, was the most exuberant of all. Glinda observed the girl running about and examining the plants, paintings, and furniture in the sorceress's dining room. She looked at Ozma, Dorothy, Betsy and Button Bright. Betsy, Dorothy, and Ozma were feeling poorly, but Button Bright was not. What did he have in common with Trot? The biggest difference he had was that his heritage was Ozian; he was a Yookoohoo. All of the children had come to settle permanently in Oz during the early part of the twentieth century, but Dorothy had been the first to arrive. Glinda considered again, realizing that Button Bright did not permanently settle in Oz until years after his first arrival. Could the duration of their time in Oz affect their health?

This train of thought was not working, so the sorceress put it aside. Still, Button Bright and Trot were more vibrant than the others, yet she was certain that whatever virus they had contracted in Flora was being carried by all four of them. And it was communicable, as well, as evidenced by Ozma's malaise. Why would a fairy be susceptible to a virus, and a Yookoohoo not?

Still, Glinda was not aware of any others exhibiting symptoms.

"Tell me," she said, addressing all five of her guests, "has anyone else complained of a headache? Your aunt and uncle, perhaps?" she added, speaking to Dorothy. "Jellia Jamb? Anyone?"

Dorothy, Trot, Betsy, Button Bright and Ozma took a few moments to consider it, but none of them were aware of anyone else feeling poorly.

Glinda sent a directive to her handmaidens that they were to monitor her Book of Records for any instance of headaches, congestion, stomach cramps, or other discomforts. Glinda herself chose to spend all her time with the children.

As they were eating a light salad and drinking iced tea, three faint trills of a whistle were heard and Herby the Medicine Man arrived.

The Medicine Man was one of Oz's more unusual inhabitants. Having been enchanted long ago by the witch Mombi, Herby's chest was constructed of a medicine cabinet, in which he kept various remedies, medicines, herbal supplements, vitamins, and tinctures. He wore a powdered wig upon his head and a broad smile upon his face.

"How may I be of service?" he asked, noting the six people he had joined. He bowed low, causing the medicine bottles in his chest to rattle, but kept his hands clasped firmly over it.

Herby was welcomed to the table, and served a salad and tea from one of Glinda's man-servants. The server was dressed in shades of yellow, indicating to the others that he was a Winkie. "You look familiar," spoke Ozma to him as the young man set a bowl of salad before Herby.

The server smiled and bowed. "I should hope so," he said. "It's me: Woot."

"But you're wearing yellow..." remarked Betsy, upon realizing with whom they spoke.

"I spent some time in the west. I really liked it there." He shrugged dismissively. "And now I'm here. Glinda was kind enough to let me work with her staff for a while. I suppose I'll pick up some red clothes if I stay here long enough."

"The wanderer is starting to settle?" asked Button Bright.

Woot smirked. "For *now*. We'll see where life takes me."

"Won't you join us?" asked Betsy. She smiled sweetly, despite the pressure in her head.

"I don't mind if I do!" replied the wanderer, looking to find another chair. The others were seated at a small table in Glinda's private living room, and the sorceress had only provided enough chairs for herself and her guests. "Let me pick up a chair from one of the others rooms," he suggested.

"Actually," interjected the sorceress, placing a hand upon Woot's forearm, "I was hoping to ask you to take a shift in the library, reading the Book of Records. I need to get all available eyes scrutinizing it. You understand, I'm sure."

Glinda figured that Betsy was only being polite; however, she did not want to take the risk of prolonged exposure to whatever virus the children were carrying.

"Of course," replied Woot, looking somewhat disappointed.

"I'm sorry. It's so very important." Glinda apologized to him and the children. "Let's have Woot join us when we return from Burzee. Shall we?"

Once Woot had departed, Glinda addressed Herby and explained the situation to him. Herby immediately withdrew three bottles of natural herbs from his medicine chest.

"Antibiotics only kill bacteria, not viruses. We can eliminate opportunistic bacterial infections, but we also need antiviral medication to take out viruses. Take these. Anti-inflammatory. Analgesic. Each of you take one of these as well." He doled out the three pills each to Ozma, Dorothy, Betsy, Trot and Button Bright. "And an immunity vitamin booster," he added, handing out a larger, mottled grey pill to each of them, as well as to Glinda and himself. "Take with a beverage." He noticed that Button Bright was about to start chewing the pills like candy, and placed his hand upon the boy's. "They won't taste very good. Place them on your tongue, and drink something to wash them down."

Herby's medicines were taken, not without a few grimaces, and the Medicine Man cast pleased looks all around. "Good, good! We'll treat the symptoms, fortify against recurrence, and work on a cure! I very much look forward to meeting Zurline and the great Ak! Won't Zim be jealous of me!" He whispered conspiringly to Ozma, "But don't worry. I plan on bringing back lots of plants and herbs. It's great to have such a wonderful botanist to work with."

The queen of Oz smiled back. She was already feeling better, and the congestion in her head had all but completely disappeared. She no longer felt queasy, and was overjoyed to see Dorothy and Betsy perking up as well.

"There, now, you see? All will be well!" exulted Herby, laughing so that the bottles in his chest rattled. "When do we depart for Burzee?" he asked of Glinda.

"First light tomorrow morning," answered Glinda, also relieved. The good witch finally felt comfortable enough to eat her own salad and drink her tea. She swallowed her food and blinked, still thinking about viruses and cures and how totally foreign such concepts were in Oz. Yet, Herby the Medicine Man existed because at one time sickness and disease did exist in Oz. She remembered those days all too well and hoped that such a time would never come again.

Her guests put to bed for the night, Glinda decided

to spend the entire night poring over the books in her library. She nodded at Woot, as he and two others filtered through the entries in the great Book of Records. Each of her servants had notebooks in which they jotted down information that they felt was pertinent enough to refer to later, or alert the sorceress about.

"Nothing yet," reported Woot, glancing up.

"You may wish to see about these other matters, though," said a Munchkin girl, handing her notebook to Glinda. "There is mention of the Hoppers and Horners being upset, and the *Crescent Moon* might be in danger."

"Red Reera the Yookoohoo has a new pet," reported a Gillikin boy, reading from his notebook. "Polychrome fell."

"Kaliko has another toothache," said a boy in green.

Among the hundreds of thousands of entries in the Great Book, it was surprising to Glinda that there were this many mentions of events that might be of interest to her. The witch was a swift reader, and turned back two pages in the book to pore over it in case the others might have missed something. Soon, she had caught up on the day, and followed along with the others as new entries appeared in the book.

As Woot and the two others grew tired, Glinda pulled a velvet cord and summoned three other readers to take their place.

"Good night," she said.

Part 2
Chapter 7
What Lies in Castle Flora

THE TEAM found themselves in the anteroom of castle Flora. All were silent, knowing full well that sudden transport would bring them to a potentially hazardous foreign situation.

Fifteen people and animals turned their attention to General Jinjur. She scanned the chamber, noting the grey stone walls, the entryways to the front and to the back, as well as three portal windows set upon each side of the chamber. Beyond the windows she could see mountains on one side, and deep night sky on the other. She wanted to get her bearing and determine her directions. From the maps that Mandy and Klaus had provided, she knew that the anteroom opened to a courtyard facing northward. Thus, with the mountainside visible on the right, it was easy to determine.

"West courtyard, eh? Indeed." Jinjur motioned Jo Files to her side, and on silent feet he neared her. She whispered, "Our first duty is to protect the troops. We must gather information. Reconnaissance. The monkey and the cats will be perfect for that."

"According to the map, we are smack dab in the middle of the castle. Outside is a courtyard. Beyond this room is the main hall of the castle. There are rooms underneath the main staircase that were used for guests." Private Files pulled out his map as he spoke to verify their position.

"About... twenty yards? Perhaps twenty yards to the south and east is a ballroom. Klaus says that it is unused."

"Are you suggesting we move the team there?" asked Jinjur.

Private Files nodded, then looked at Tik-Tok, Stampedro, Benny, and Captain Fyter. The mechanical man's whirring and clicking resounded in the anteroom, and alarmed the general. Jinjur cast a severe look at Zim, who nodded and held up a finger.

The tall wizard and his wife darted swiftly to Tik-Tok. Maggie held Zim's satchel open and he reached in to retrieve a phial of white crystal powder. This he sprinkled over the copper man, and within seconds not a sound came from Tik-Tok's mechanisms. Zim nodded assuredly at Jinjur, then followed her gaze to the living statue and the Tin Soldier.

"Step forward," ordered Zim after sprinkling the powder on Benny's feet. The statue did as told. He smiled when his movement made no sound.

"Everyone," ordered Jinjur, pointing her gloved finger around at the assemblage.

All of the boots and feet were sprinkled with the powder, completely depleting the wizard's supply. He finished with his own and Maggie's, then shook out the last upon Jinjur's own boots.

Private Files conferred with the Cowardly Lion, Hungry Tiger, and Kak. He gave them instructions to skulk about the shadows and explore the immediate vicinity of the castle interior. To Kak he handed a set of maps.

"There is little time to study this. Take it with you. Do not go far," he ordered to each of them. "Always have an escape route. We go now to the ballroom. If that is secure, then I want the three of you to fan out and discover what you can."

Kak, the Lion and the Tiger each nodded, silent.

"You're terrified." The Hungry Tiger did not ask; rather, he informed his friend. Being feline, both animals had strong senses, and though the others likely did not know it, the Cowardly Lion was trembling and his breath came in sharp gasps.

The great cat nodded to his friend, though he did not speak. Instead, the Tiger continued.

"Control yourself. This is no time to be afraid."

Gulping, the Lion finally spoke. "I'll s-save it for after, th-then." He was more terrified than he had ever been, but he recalled the courage that the Wizard had given him so many years ago, when he, Dorothy, Toto, the Scarecrow and the Tin Woodman first met. He let his breath out, took a deep one in, and set his shoulders. "I'm good," he said, quietly.

The team moved south in the anteroom to the doorway that led to the castle proper. A fresh wooden bolt and bars had been fastened to it. The children had reported that the bolt had been destroyed when they escaped with Terrence, Christian and Klaus.

"They work fast here," commented Notta Bit More. He frowned, pulling his lips down in exaggeration.

"...for a castle with only a king and a few guards," muttered Prince Corum. He laid his hand upon his horse's back as they waited for Benny to lift the bolt.

"Something is definitely amiss here," added Stampedro. He wanted to paw at the floor with his hoof, but thought better of it, even though he knew that his footfalls would be silent.

Benny stepped forward at Jinjur's orders and placed his hands underneath the heavy wooden bolt. Lifting it was simple for him, and he did it silently. Holding it in his hands, he stepped back. "I will hold onto this," he said, carefully hefting it over his shoulder. It looked to Jinjur to weigh at least sixty pounds. The wood was fresh, and the bolt was thick. She wondered how many of Gorsbenor's men it took to lift into place.

Jinjur held up a hand for pause. "Halt," she hissed. She turned to Files and Notta. "Why would the castle be bolted from the outside? We are in the anteroom. That means we are technically outside of the castle. If the king and his troops are inside, then why would the castle entrance be bolted from out here?"

"Wait," urged Files, turning back to the others. He, Jinjur and Notta were at the head of the group, standing immediately behind Benny. The advance halted, and everyone remained stationary where they stood. Private Files turned back to Jinjur. The last time he had been in an abandoned castle, there was foul magic afoot. It nearly cost him his beloved wife, Ozga. It was only with the benevolent intervention of Zim and his assistant Dinny that Files was able to rescue his wife and disenchant the entire castle. This situation was different. The castle and its inhabitants were not enchanted. It was much, much worse.

Jinjur held her finger to her lips, raising her right arm. With everyone's attention, she lowered her hand to grasp the sword at her waist and unsheathe it.

The whispers of steel against metal sounded like a strong wind through a forest of trees. Handy Mandy wielded three spears, three swords, and a shield. Corum raised his own shield and brandished his sword. Captain Fyter shouldered his musket, having no need for a shield.

Their defensive stances enabled, Jinjur nodded.

With his free hand, Benny grasped one of the iron bars fastened to the door and pulled it. The ancient metal hinges creaked loud and angrily.

Gritting her teeth, General Jinjur stepped forward, her sword and shield at the ready.

Beyond the door, what met their sight was nothing any of them had ever seen before.

The entire entry of the castle was filled with men and women. They stood shoulder-to-shoulder, silent and unmoving. Even when the ante-room door was opened, not a single one of them moved. Jinjur could see that they were all unkempt and dirty, with dark smears of filth on their faces and arms.

"They don't breathe," whispered Notta. The skin on his arms prickled as each hair rose, sending shivers down his spine.

All of the visitors were tensed for combat. They had their weapons and shields ready. Their bodies were taut and ready to spring. But the crowd of people behind the opened door was immobile. Furthermore, their backs were turned to the anteroom, and it appeared that not a single one of them noticed the newcomers.

Some of the people shuffled or wobbled, and occasionally there would be a twitch or other sort of movement. One of those closest to the anteroom door slowly moved to notice the group. The man stared unblinkingly at them, his mouth hanging agape. As militant and rigid as Jinjur was, she nearly let loose a gasp. The man looked terrible. His eyes were deeply sunk into their sockets, as were his cheeks. Worse, his nose was completely gone, leaving a pit in the middle of his face in which they could see portions of his skull. The skin of his face was mottled brown and black, and what they thought was filth was actually his own decayed flesh.

"Close. The. Door." The hissed directive came from Jo Files through gritted teeth. There was no more silence powder from Zim, so Benny did his best to close the door as quietly as possible. Just as he swung the massive oaken door shut, a dark shape darted past the statue's head and disappeared into the darkness.

"What was that?" demanded General Jinjur as loudly as she dared. "Report!"

"I... I'm not sure, General," mumbled Jo Files, his glance furtively passing over all the people assembled in the anteroom. "I... I think those were people. But..." He counted all in attendance but one. "Kak is gone."

"Good," Jinjur replied, her eyes steadily planted on the oaken door. "At least one of us acted." The winged monkey gained much favor with the general for his action, and she hoped her esteem of the simian was well-placed.

"They didn't move," commented Notta, moving close to the general.

Jinjur ignored him and addressed Benny, Tik-Tok, and the Tin Soldier. "The three of you. To the door. Fortify it. Get the bolt back on there, and lean against it. You will not let *any*one back in." Including Kak, she added, silently.

To the Lion and the Tiger, she spoke next. "The two of you will perform reconnaissance outside. To the courtyard." She led the great cats to the northern doorway, and found it was bolted as well. Motioning to Corum, Private Files, and Handy Mandy, she ordered them to lift the bolt.

Mandy stepped forward, waving back the two men at her side. "I got this," she said with a smirk. Using all seven of her arms, the goat girl from Mount Mern hefted the bolt upward and off the metal frames.

The Yellow Knight carefully pulled the door away from its hinges, revealing an empty courtyard underneath a dark midnight sky. Jinjur pointed at the great cats and directed them to exit. She then gestured at Tommy Kwikstep and Perry, directing them to come close to her.

"The two of you follow the Lion and the Tiger. Give them five minutes. If there is nothing, then you will go out and continue checking the perimeter. I want the courtyard secured. Tommy, you're the fastest runner I know. Perry, you will keep up with him and make sure you do not stray far. Zim," she added, waving the sorcerer to her. "We discussed a barrier in last night's meeting. Do you have it ready?"

"I do," replied the sorcerer, turning to his wife. Maggie, ever vigilant, had his satchel ready and raised it for the tall wizard to reach into. He withdrew five tripods, one at a time, and handed them to Handy Mandy, who Jinjur had waved to join them.

As Tommy and Perry silently exited the front anteroom door, the group began to slowly dwindle in size. "Clown," Jinjur spoke to Notta Bit More, "you and the knight will join Mandy in setting up a perimeter. The courtyard is five-sided. These tripods will be set up in each corner of the courtyard." She glanced up at Benny, who, with Tik-Tok and Captain Fyter, appeared to be relaxing in front of the southern doorway. She debated if she could afford to remove him from that position. Taking a gamble, she whispered at him. "I want you to go outside and find boulders. Bring them in here—*quietly!*—and barricade that door. I need all my troops mobile."

The statue nodded, and swiftly strode forward and past the huddled Ozian troops. He followed Mandy, Notta, and Corum out the northern doorway, leaving Jinjur with only Fyter, Tik-Tok, Zim, Maggie, Jo Files, and Stampedro.

Within minutes, Benny returned with a massive boulder held in his strong arms, which he effortlessly set down in front of the castle entrance. "More," ordered Jinjur. "Are there more to bring?"

Benny nodded, saluted, and strode out of the castle once again.

Out in the pentagonal courtyard, Corum, Notta and Mandy had positioned their tripods in each segmented corner. The sky was clear, and enough stars were visible to light their task. Once the tripods were set up, they returned to the anteroom to await further orders.

Jinjur directed Zim and Maggie to activate the magical barriers, and followed them outside to observe their success.

Zim, for all his confidence, found himself facing a challenge. In Flora, despite the name, there appeared to be not a single plant visible. The courtyard was bereft of vegetation—even withered. Not a single bloom or leaf could he sense. Just stone. No matter. He derived much of his magic from the green, but innately Zim was a sorcerer, with his own stores. He grasped his wife's hand. Maggie was a witch with her own magical abilities. Together they could do this. It was a contingency they had prepared for, but were hoping would not present itself.

Starting with the tripod situated at the anteroom entrance, Zim and Maggie placed their hands upon it, chanted the words to a spell, and focused their energies into it. Minutes ticked by and Jinjur did not detect anything happening as a result of their efforts. A bead of perspiration appeared on her forehead, and she quickly brushed it away. She gritted her teeth and clenched her hands into fists. "Make it work!" she whispered under her breath.

Zim and Maggie were frowning in concentration, and it appeared as if a great physical strain was put upon them. Maggie licked her dry lips and glared angrily at the tripod upon which their hands were gripped. She looked at her husband, nodded, and the two of them repeated the chant.

A gentle green glow surrounded the first tripod, bursting into a green flame that lit up that corner of the courtyard. Smiling with relief, the Greenleafs nodded to Jinjur, then strode to the next tripod. The general could not help but notice a look of disappointment on the tall wizard's face as he turned. Was the flame not strong enough? It appeared to be working.

It took longer than they expected to activate all five tripods, and by the time Maggie led her tall husband back to Jinjur, both were visibly exhausted. In that same time, Benny had retrieved six more boulders, which he positioned inside the anteroom and against the doorway to the castle.

"Fall in," hissed the general, loud enough for everyone to hear.

Except for the Lion, Tiger, Perry, Tommy and Kak, the entire team awaited General Jinjur's next orders. Jinjur turned to Notta, and spoke directly to him. "What now?" she asked. Their initial plan would not work. They could not set up a stronghold in the castle ballroom. Their stronghold was now the open courtyard. She now made use of Notta's scheming mind.

The clown, realizing it was up to him to come up with a plan, blanched whiter. "Ahem," he coughed. He reached into his coat and retrieved the maps that Mandy had provided each of them with. With shaking hands, the clown began scrutinizing the papers.

General Jinjur's gloved hand closed around his wrist, steadying him. "I need you at one hundred percent, clown," she ordered.

The clown gripped the maps tight. "Right then. The anteroom is no longer an entrance to the castle. The wizard's tower is destroyed." He turned to the side-view map of the castle and the mountain crag it was situated upon. "Is the courtyard secured?"

Jinjur glanced at Zim, who nodded. "Yes."

"From the courtyard, down the northern mountain slope, is a trail leading to a village where the king's subjects live. West of us is a crag. East of us is a cliff that falls down to a valley. We can presume that Gorsbenor and his... er, people... are holed up in the castle. No aid will be coming from the village. In fact, we are here to aid anyone who's left." The clown scrunched up his face in thought. "We've got a perimeter. The anteroom is fortified. We have troops. The people in the castle are not doing a thing. We can sweep through and locate Gorsbenor. Subdue him. Once we have the head of the snake, we can put an end to whatever he is doing, and reverse the damage."

"How do you propose we do that?" asked Jo Files, speaking out of turn and disgruntling General Jinjur, who glared at him.

"I'm not certain. All we know is that Gorsbenor is in the castle." Notta pointed to the map, indicating the king's bedchamber and suite. "We move through the people in the castle. We get to the villain. We take him down. Once he is immobile, we proceed from there."

"I need a plan, clown," insisted Jinjur. They had gone over scenarios back in the Emerald City, but all of their planning seemed to fly out the window with the situation they found themselves in. She asked, "How do we *know* he is in the castle?"

"Those... *people* are in the castle entry. Klaus informed us that he was doing things to the people to create an army. They are obviously his army. The leader of an army would not be far from his troops."

"Good point," agreed Jinjur. She noticed the Cowardly Lion and Hungry Tiger returning. "That makes sense. Proceed."

"The courtyard is secure," repeated the clown. "So is the anteroom. We have a foothold on the castle invasion. From what I saw, there were anywhere from fifty to one hundred people standing in the castle. There are sixteen of us. We have weapons and strength. I propose we remove the boulders, push through the crowd, and get to the king's chambers."

"Simple as that, eh?" asked Jinjur, following along with the plan. She admired the clown's plan, but worried that their target would not be where they expected, and knew that he would not be without protection. "What do we do if he isn't there? What if he's guarded?"

"We have weapons and shields," replied Notta, his eyes darting as the plan came about in his head. "If the king is not there, then we sweep through the castle until we locate him. According to the map there are five levels below the castle. We start at the top, move downward. Don't forget:

we have a winged monkey in there. He has a map. If he's as smart as I hope he is, he's already been searching the castle."

Jinjur wondered why Tommy and Perry had not yet returned, then returned her attention to the clown. "Then what?" Despite being a general, she loved her son greatly, and was beginning to grow concerned.

Notta scowled at Jinjur. "We subdue the king. That's the goal. Subdue him. Reverse what he's done. Leave. Send the refugees back."

Jinjur regarded Notta with stern eyes. "All right then." She turned to the others. "Benny. I want you to clear the boulders from the door. Leave them on each side so we can barricade it if we need to. Tik-Tok, Captain Fyter. You two will lead. We head to the stairwell, then up."

She pointed to Mandy. "Have your weapons ready. All of you. We follow behind and sweep upward, then downward."

To Maggie and Zim, she directed, "You two will remain here with Benny and Stampedro. This is our safe room, and the courtyard is our retreat. Set up a triage to treat injuries."

"*If* we have injuries?" queried Notta.

"*When* we have injuries." Jinjur glared at him. "We are in unfamiliar territory. Lurline's enchantment does not appear to extend here. We do not know what we will encounter. That was made clear to you all every step of the way."

The clown, chastened, nodded and looked downward.

The plan was set in motion. Benny removed the boulders and situated them on either side of the anteroom's southern entrance. He hefted the bolt and opened the door as before. Like previously, the crowd of people in the castle entry did not move, even though it appeared as if some noticed the Ozians. Taking heart, Jinjur led the team carefully through the doorway.

The crowd was unmoving, but were easily parted out of the Ozians' path. Tik-Tok, tightly wound, led with Captain Fyter. The metal men were easily able to push the people aside. They appeared docile and complacent. Many of the Ozians noticed with extreme discomfort that bits of flesh fell from the people where Fyter's axe handle or Tik-Tok's hands pushed at them.

As much as they wanted to skirt the subject, they were all very well aware of what Klaus had told them about his work. Necromancy meant magic utilizing the dead. That meant that all the people they were pushing past were dead. Animated, but dead.

"Shields up," ordered Jinjur. She did not wish to touch any of the people, and despite her militant stance, she did not wish to harm them either. These people were victims. "They *are* victims," she whispered aloud.

As they moved closer to the grand stairwell, the crowd of undead became thicker and their progress slowed. The people began to grunt and murmur incoherently.

Goosebumps ran up and down General Jinjur's arms. She and the others came to Flora expecting battle. What they got in exchange was more than eerie, more than disturbing. What they got was an unmoving army of victims. Drawing her face down in distaste, Jinjur sheathed her sword and tightened her grip on her shield.

"Huhh," spoke a voice to her right, and Jinjur was shocked to see a woman looking directly at her. The woman's face was nearly rotted away, exposing the skull in patches. Her lower jaw was gone, and her tongue lolled downward like a hideous necktie.

Jinjur covered her mouth to suppress a shriek. The woman made no move to stop her, and was soon shoved out of her sight by the bodies of other victims.

The general's heart was beating fast in her chest. Her son and his partner were outside somewhere, and that worried her. She wanted to calm herself by breathing deeply, but the odor of decay and death was all about them. Its pungency permeated the room. She wrinkled her nose and looked forward, following the metal men as they got closer to the stairwell.

It took them only twenty minutes to pass through the crowd, but to the troops it felt like an eternity. Upon encountering the grand staircase, they were able to ascend it unimpeded. Reaching the second level, all those that could be were breathless.

"I need wind-ing," spoke Tik-Tok mechanically. "It would be ter-rib-le for me to run down in this sit-u-a-tion."

The mechanical man's words were precise, and communicated what they all realized to be true. Mandy wound Tik-Tok's gears swiftly, but this was no time or place for any of them to refuel. They had all eaten before leaving the Emerald City. If all went well, then they would be returning to Oz before anyone could even think of being hungry.

"Can't find him!" A blur of dark brown fur and feathers caught General Jinjur's attention as Kak emerged from the shadows above the staircase. "There's nobody up there. At all." The winged monkey landed, breathless, on the top railing of the stairwell. He looked down at the mass of undead and stifled a retch. "There's nobody up there. No one. I checked everywhere. The rooms are all empty."

Jinjur nodded. With great chagrin, she realized that they would need to once again pass through the people in order to travel to the lower levels of the castle. It was the next place for them to search.

She turned to Notta. "The servant's tunnels," she said. "Lead us to the nearest one." Her mind was racing as she tried to balance her attention to the mission with her worry over her missing son.

The clown nodded. "Prince Terrence's chamber. It's over this way," he said, pointing down a hallway to the east. As the Ozians neared it, they were met with a battering ram tossed haphazardly partway between the hallway and the chamber. The door was shattered. No effort had been made to clear the debris.

"This is it," spoke Notta. He stepped forward and entered the room, jumping over the battering ram. The others followed, and once inside they pushed aside the shelf that led to the tunnel. It was large enough for each of them to enter, and Jinjur was glad that she made the more cumbersome members of the crew remain behind.

"One at a time," she hissed. "Tik-Tok. You remain here as guard." She ushered the rest of them into the tunnel, the Lion and Tiger at the lead.

Thankfully there was no conversation for her to keep track of. She had ordered them all to hold their tongues unless they had something pertinent to say.

Torches were appropriated from sconces on the hallway walls. In their firelight, the tunnel led them swiftly to the kitchen located in the basement of the castle. From there, they all trooped to the scullery, where the tunnel to the lower level had been left open. Apparently the king's troops had not thought to close it behind them after they had raided it. Indeed, there was no need to.

The maps that Klaus provided were invaluable in this situation. Once again Jinjur went over the schematic in her mind. She had memorized it, and directed the others to do their best to memorize it. The same tunnel that led to the dungeons led downward to the catacombs.

A growl from the Hungry Tiger up ahead caught their attention. The Cowardly Lion joined his friend in growling.

"Monkey," ordered Jinjur. "What is going on? Find out."

Kak flitted forward to see what was disturbing the cats. A simian shriek carried back to Jinjur. She raised her hand to halt their progress. She moved past Private Files and the two metal men, then past the Cowardly Lion. In front of her, the Hungry Tiger's hackles were raised. His purple fur stood on end as his back arched. Her sword sheathed and her shield upon her back, the general placed her hand upon the Tiger's back and moved forward, torch in hand. She chose to withdraw her sword, careful to protect the Tiger from it.

Beyond the large head of the great cat, a miserable sight met Jinjur's eyes. "Oh," she uttered in disgust. From the descriptions that Terrence, Klaus and Christian had given, Lon Gorsbenor was an overweight, short man, older, with dark hair and a mustache. The crown on his head was another indication.

Gorsbenor's body lay, unmoving, in the hallway at their feet. Jinjur nudged him with her boot, but he did not react. "Is he breathing?" asked the general of the Tiger.

"No," spoke the animal after lowering his head to sniff at the man. "He stinks. But he's not breathing."

Jinjur regarded the body of Terrence's uncle. This presented yet another change to their plans. They located the king—rather, the prince regent—and he was dead. The people of Flora were gathered in the castle, also dead, but animated.

"What killed him?" demanded the general. "Clown. Private. Up front!"

Files and Notta joined her in regarding the corpse. "What do you make of this?" Not waiting for an answer, she knelt and started prodding at the former tyrant with her gloved hand. She looked up. "Come on. We need to find out what killed him."

"That," commented the clown. His face was contorted and he looked as if he were about to cry. He pointed at the king's head, which lolled sideways as Jinjur poked at his body.

A jagged bone was protruding from the man's head, right above his left ear. Below that, smaller bone fragments were embedded in his head and neck. Dried up blood had clotted in several abrasions.

"Look at his hands." Jo Files indicated the dead man's hands, which were curled around more bone fragments. "He was pulling them out." He looked at the massive bone sticking out of the man's back. "And that one there. I don't know how he planned to pull that one out."

"My guess is that he came here on his own, tried to pull out these bones, and perished." Notta closed his eyes, an expression of great sadness upon his clown face.

Jinjur was still examining the body. "So we know he was... murdered. What we don't know is who did this to him, correct?"

Notta and the great cats assented.

"From what I know of death, once a body dies, it begins to decay. We saw that several of the undead people in the castle were doing just that. The longer they are not alive, the more they decay. This man has not decayed. That means he died recently." She looked up at the others, an eyebrow raised. "Do we agree on that?"

Files and Notta nodded, as did the Hungry Tiger.

Jinjur cleared her throad. "All right then. We proceed to the catacombs. Then we sweep up."

Stepping over the body, Jinjur and the others continued downward until they emerged in the dungeon.

The next two hours found the troop of Ozians trekking downward to the very base of Castle Flora. During that time they encountered not a single soul, living or dead. The level below the dungeon contained a store of weapons. Swords, spears, knives and morningstars littered the room. In the lowest level they discovered the disturbed resting places of the castle ancestors. In several instances coffins had been opened, and as they suspected, all were empty.

No evidence existed of any terrible dangers chained in the catacombs, as Klaus had warned them of. Whatever had been down there was no longer confined to the dungeon, and that did not sit well with the general.

The Ozians trudged back upward, using the castle's stairways between levels. It was completely bereft of anyone. There was no evidence of anyone or anything residing in the castle.

In confusion and discouragement, Jinjur led her team to the kitchen cellars and then back up to the main hallway. As before, it was bustling with the undead.

They emerged from a doorway behind the grand staircase, immediately pushing aside several undead.

"I do not understand," sighed the exasperated general, throwing up her hands. "What is going on here?" Her voice rose as she spoke, causing the undead to shuffle about and look her way. She wanted to cry out for her son, but held her tongue.

General Jinjur and her troops had lowered their defenses, based on their initial interaction with the undead. They had no reason to believe that there would be any interference.

They were wrong.

• • •

Perry and Tommy ran as quietly as they could. Years of military training had strengthened Perry, and both had attended Professor Wogglebug's College of Athletic Training and Perfection.

The cold night air filled their lungs as they ran, side by side. Beyond the courtyard a path wound around the base of the castle. Without speaking, Tommy headed for it, even though it descended into shadows. Perry followed, his breathing steady as they jogged downward.

"Not too far," said Jinjur's son as they ran. "We just need to know—"

"Our immediate surroundings," said Tommy, finishing the sentence for him. "Right." He kept going, rounding the foundation of the castle. The rocky base of the castle was rough, but clearly the path had seen use, for it was worn smooth in parts, with sand filling crevices. There were even small seashells among the sand, which they could glimpse as the shadows were broken by starlight in places.

After running ten minutes, striding around the base of the castle, they could see a valley below, and a steep drop-off. The path continued to wind around the castle, but it dropped further down, wrapped in darkness and shadow.

"We should head back," said Tommy. They had stopped whispering as they found nothing but barren stone around the castle. There was no sign of habitation whatsoever.

"All right. My mother—"

Tommy glanced at his partner. He had heard a sound not unlike a gust of wind, or the sound of an arrow being shot. Perry stood motionless, his eyes agog, holding his hand to his throat.

"What is it?" he asked, timidly placing his hand on Perry's forearm. He felt the need to pull his partner's arm downward. He needed to see why he was holding his hand against his throat. Perry resisted, and Tommy's breathing caught in his lungs. Blood was beginning to seep between Perry's fingers. Tommy stopped breathing altogether as goosebumps traveled up and down his arms.

"We need to go. Now." Tommy tugged on Perry's arm, but the son of General Jinjur was rooted to the spot. "Come on. Please." The former messenger pulled desperately, then froze in fear as a low growl came from the shadows and the same sound whispered past his ear. He ducked away from it, and saw a bone fragment bounce off the castle foundation behind him. Turning to Perry, he saw his dear friend's legs start to crumble beneath him, and—reacting quickly—was able to catch him as he fell.

"Oh, no. No. No no no," he muttered as Perry leaned heavily on him. Something big was moving in the dark shadows ahead of them, and Tommy clearly heard chains being dragged. Whatever it was, it was getting closer.

Another bone fragment shot through the air, impaling itself into his shoulder. Tommy cried out in pain. With Perry in his arms, he was unable to pull the jagged bone out.

"Perry, we need to go. Please, we need to leave. Now. We have to go."

As the sound of chains and groaning got closer, both young men could see a dark shape lumbering upward toward them. This time, a volley of bone fragments shot toward them, hitting Perry in the back and side, and hitting

Tommy's arm and the back of his neck.

"Augh!" he cried out. He did his best to steady Perry next to him, then reached up his other arm to pull the bones out of himself and his partner. His breathing was ragged, and he was beginning to see spots in front of his eyes. He looked tenderly at Perry, who still clamped his hand to his neck.

Breathing heavily, Tommy Kwickstep looked upward at the thing that was emerging from the shadows, and found his own legs turning to jelly beneath him.

Not fifteen feet away from them was a large undead man with chains shackled about his feet. He was easily the largest person that either of them had ever seen, rivaling giants back in Oz. He had to be at least ten feet tall, and nearly as wide around. The chains dragged behind him as he lurched forward. He was heavily muscled, and would have been an imposing sight in life. In death, the man's girth was slowly rotting away.

What terrified them both was the fact that this man— rather, this undead man—had clenched in each massive hand several skeletal arms and legs. As he moved, the creature grabbed handfuls of finger and leg bones, tore them off, and hurled them at Tommy and Perry.

Crying out as even more bone shards tore into their flesh, Tommy found himself crouching down in terror, with Perry still clutched in his arms.

"S-sword," gurgled Perry, his eyes urgently pleading with Tommy. "Don't give up."

Part 2
Chapter 8
The Council of Eld

GLINDA, Ozma, Herby, Dorothy, Trot, Betsy, and Button Bright were welcomed to the forest of Burzee by a throng of elder fairies. Their wings flitted about them as the ethereal creatures guided Glinda's swan chariot to land in a clearing. The birds touched down with delicate finesse and settled instantly.

Glinda had no worries that the swans would fly off. They had made this trip many times before. She loosened the reins on the birds and allowed them to wander about and enjoy the clearing. Upon disembarking the chariot, the people were escorted without pause toward a trail in the forest.

In moments the fairies led them to another clearing. Gathered in this clearing, seated upon various thrones made from tree stumps, large mushrooms, and even thick bushes, was the council of elders among the forest. The great Ak, Queen Zurline, and even Santa Claus was present. Several knooks and ryls dashed about, and other fairies wandered in and out of the clearing to see what was going on.

Zurline welcomed the Ozians, rising and holding out her arms. "My friends," she said, smiling grandly at them. "It is so good to see you." She glanced back at the great Ak, who rose and joined her.

"Children," spoke the master woodsman of the world. He put his hand underneath Dorothy's chin and lifted her face to his. The Kansas girl smiled at him, comforted by the tenderness in Ak's eyes. "What has bedeviled you?" He placed a hand on Zurline's arm. "Have a look. Tell me what you see."

Zurline tenderly placed her hand on Dorothy's cheek. A look of concern crossed her lovely features. She repeated the movement upon Ozma, Betsy, Trot and Button Bright. A troubled frown crossed the lovely queen's face, and she closed her eyes. She appeared to be confused, then frustrated. "I need a moment," she murmured, returning to her throne. Instead of sitting, she remained standing. Zurline turned to regard the children, scrutinizing each of them in turn.

Herby, nervous to be in the presence of such luminaries, raised a hand and spoke. "I... I, er... I have been treating them. Their symptoms include headache, nausea, stomach cramps, and dizziness."

Zurline regarded the medicine man and nodded to him. "Your help is *greatly* appreciated," she replied, smiling sincerely. "For that, you will be rewarded. For now, please join us as we confer. Glinda? Will you join us as well?"

Glinda and Herby both nodded, stepping forward to enter the closed circle of elders. Zurline turned back to the children. "Please, relax and enjoy the forest. A meal is waiting for you. We will return soon. All will be well."

Ozma and the other children were brought to another clearing, where several fairy folk showered them with treats. A large table was set in the center, with wooden chairs set about it in a circle. Bowls of berries, cups of water and tea and fruit juices, and sandwiches made from delicate green leaves and thick mushrooms, filled with nuts and berries.

Their repast was short lived. They had not taken but their first bites of the sandwiches when the knooks, ryls and fairies began chattering excitedly. "Oh!" cried Ozma with a smile as Zurline, Ak, Santa Claus, Glinda and Herby joined them. The elders and their friends joined them at the meal, and were served the same sandwiches and drinks.

"You all have a virus," spoke Ak softly. He drank from a goblet, and licked his lips. "I should say, you all *had* a virus. Thanks to our friend Herby, and the food you have consumed, the virus has been eradicated from your bodies. Finish your food." He smiled, watching as the children greedily began gobbling the food laid out before them.

Santa Claus laughed heartily, lightening the mood substantially. Smiles were shared all around, and soon Dorothy, Betsy, and Ozma were laughing and talking with their hosts.

After the meal, Glinda sighed and spoke. "We are grateful for your help." She pursed her lips and looked at the children. "You said that they had a virus. How did they contract it? And what can we do to stop it?"

A stormy look crossed over Ak's face. He looked at Zurline and Santa Claus. "All I can tell is that it was *given* to you. Specifically. This was no accidental exposure."

"As I have already said, you were cursed," added Zurline sadly, looking downward at her bare feet. "This was done to you intentionally."

Ozma gasped. "What? Who would dare?"

"And how *could* anyone...?" began Dorothy, then paled as a look of realization passed over her face. "Klaus," she muttered to Ozma, slowly turning to face her friend.

"Yes? What do you mean?" asked Santa Claus.

"No," said Trot, her eyes round and scared. "She said Klaus."

"What makes you say that?" asked the girl ruler. She did not want to believe that someone she had granted asylum to could possible betray her hospitality.

"Think about it," added Button Bright, remaining calm and collected. "He himself has admitted that he used to practice dark arts… black magic. He was also a healer. Who else knows about diseases and sicknesses but someone who cured them?"

"When all other possibilities are eliminated, what's left is the truth," spoke Ak, a grim look upon his face. "Are you certain this visitor is good? Could he not be evil?"

Ozma clamped her hands over her mouth. "He's in the Emerald City." Goosebumps covered their arms and legs as the girl ruler and Glinda rose with the others. "We have to get back!"

"There's no time to waste," spoke Ak commandingly. "I will accompany them," he said to Zurline and Santa Claus. "This matter will be resolved immediately. I have no patience for such nonsense!"

Glinda gathered several sandwiches, wrapped them in large leaves that were being used as mats, and hastily stuffed them into a pocket in her gown. "These might come in useful," she explained to Herby, who caught onto her idea and grabbed all the remaining sandwiches, stuffed them into his chest, and fastened the latch securely.

In great haste, Glinda led the way to the clearing where the swans were foraging about the brush. "Back to your stations, my dears! Please hurry!" The sorceress of the south ushered the birds to their reins and secured them fast. Ak, seeing what she was doing, joined her and soon all of the birds were ready to fly.

"Get in!" Ozma clamored from the chariot, waving her friend and the woodsman to join them. She looked at Glinda, Ak, and then at the children. "I'm so sorry my friends. Please stay here. The swans..."

Ak nodded, realizing that his added weight would be too much for the swans to handle. He turned to Button Bright and Trot. "To me, children," he said, gathering the boy and girl in his arms. He lifted them to his chest, sat them on his shoulders, and nodded to Ozma, Glinda, Dorothy, Betsy and Herby. "We shall see you in the Emerald City."

Part 2
Chapter 9
Subterfuge

THE FIRST UNDEAD to raise its voice was in the middle of the crowd. It uttered an unintelligible growl, then turned toward the visitors, throwing himself in their direction.

With a roar like thunder, the entire crowd of undead people surged toward the grand staircase, closing in on General Jinjur and her army.

"To arms!" shouted Jinjur. "Defend yourselves! We need to get to the anteroom!"

Swords and spears were drawn, and shields held outward. Hundreds of hands reached out and tore at them, and the wave of undead threatened to crush them. The Lion and the Tiger both used their great weight and strength to push forward, but against such a massive throng their effort made little headway.

With a snarl, General Jinjur began thrusting outward with her sword. Victims or not, these people were threatening to hurt and damage them, or worse. There would be no casualties under her leadership. None! The laws of this dimension were not the laws of Oz, and with a whoop, the strong woman dashed pell-mell into the assault.

Seeing her example, Private Files, Prince Corum, and Handy Mandy joined her. Swords were slashing, and spears thrust into the mass of undead attackers. With the added defensive attack, General Jinjur was able to move her troops to the anteroom entrance, from which Benny and Stampedro were launching an attack against the undead that were closest to them. From above, Kak pounced and scratched at any of the undead he could encounter without getting caught himself.

Captain Fyter and Tik Tok pushed through at the head of the group. The undead grasping at them found only cold metal, and the sharp blade of the Tin Soldier's bayonet.

With such opposition, getting to the anteroom was an extreme challenge. It took all their effort to defend themselves and move to the secure area. With Benny and Stampedro ushering them in, aided by the Lion, Tiger, Tik-Tok and Fyter, the team found themselves once again in the anteroom.

"Barricade!" ordered Jinjur.

With the bolted door straining against the onslaught of the undead, Benny rolled the boulders against it. The noise from the castle was deafening, despite the wall and the boulders.

"To the courtyard," General Jinjur ordered.

"It was a trap," cried out Notta, finding his voice. The clown looked around at his companions. "This was a trap!"

"What is happening?" demanded Zim. He and Maggie had remained behind while Benny and Stampedro entered the fray.

"The whole thing was a trap," claimed Notta, repeating what he had said earlier. He faced Jinjur. "This was a trap. We need to get back to the Emerald City."

"The charms!" cried out Mandy. She withdrew her cap from her coat pocket and held it in front of her. She looked to Jinjur for permission.

The general, breathing heavily, nodded. "Do it!" Silently, Jinjur was going frantic, concerned for her son and Tommy.

Mandy repeated the words of the spell, holding her cap in front of her. She looked at the cap, then at the others. Nothing was happening.

"Say it again," ordered Zim. "Let me hear you say the words."

Mandy spoke. "Our mission is true, victory is ours. We shall not bend to any powers. No more fighting, no more claws. It's time to return, our home is Oz."

As before, nothing happened.

"Try it!" ordered General Jinjur to Prince Corum. The yellow knight repeated the words, grasping his red feather. Tik-Tok did the same. Neither of them was successful.

"What is going on here?" demanded General Jinjur. The roaring of the undead throng beyond the wall was deafening, and she turned to glare at the barricaded door. Her eyes nearly bulged from her head as she saw the heavy stone bricks of the wall begin to crumble under the weight of the undead.

"Move people!" she shouted, pointing at the wall and then at the northern entrance. "To the courtyard!"

"They're coming!" shrieked Mandy. All seven of her arms were up in the air, each holding either a sword, shield or spear. "Run!"

Nothing else needed to be said. As a unit the team sprinted for the main entrance of the anteroom and out into the courtyard.

"Will the barrier hold?" demanded Jinjur of Zim, who had scooped up his diminutive wife and carried her in his arms.

"They will," replied Maggie, speaking for Zim. "But we don't know how long. The magic is weak here."

"No plants," huffed Zim. "No green."

"Move, people!" ordered Jinjur, repeating the words she had used before. "Move!"

The pentagonal courtyard was bathed in a green glow as the tripods burned, spreading their green flame between them.

"Head for the road," directed Jo Files, pointing to a paved path that led downward from the courtyard, then split upward up a hillside and down to the valley below.

"Up!" suggested Notta to the general, who nodded emphatically. "They'll overwhelm us if we head down!"

"Get on!" Stampedro neared Zim and Maggie. The tall sorcerer placed his wife on the horse's saddle as they came to a bottle-neck inside the anteroom, everyone trying to get out of the one northern door. Zim looked behind them at the southern door, and saw that the bricks in the wall were being pushed outward from the inside. The first of the large stones making up the wall came toppling outward, and hands began groping about the opening. The large brick above it fell loose, and was also pushed into the anteroom.

Zim wasted no time in jumping onto the horse, behind his wife. The Ozians were funneling through the door, and in minutes only Benny, the horse and his riders remained in the anteroom.

"Move!" ordered the living statue. Though his face remained, for the most part, expressionless, Benny's eyes gleamed of urgency. He stared meaningfully at them, then slapped Stampedro's flank. The horse took off in a gallop, causing Zim to duck down low over Maggie as they surged out of the anteroom. Benny watched them depart, then slowly turned his neck to regard the emerging throng of undead that cascaded into the anteroom. He raised an eyebrow, turned back to the north door, and began walking.

The undead, not sensing any life from the statue, began dashing past him, ignoring the man of stone in their mad dash to pursue the others.

Benny stretched his arms out to the side, catching several undead in their heads, and knocking several clean off their necks. A massive wooden door bolt lay alongside the door, which he surmised have have been a spare. "This will do," he muttered, bending down to pick it up. The statue, though seemingly unfeeling, scowled in disgust. He felt another emotion as he walked forward, pummeling several undead in his path with the wooden beam. Benny could not discern if the emotion he felt was disappointment, sadness, despair, disgust, or a combination of them all. The statue felt another feeling that he never expected to experience. He felt tired. Benny shook his head to clear the sand from it and continued swinging the bolt, making a sheer mess of the former people who were now filling the anteroom.

As the living statue emerged, he saw that the courtyard was empty of his compatriots, but filled to overflowing with the undead. Stone planters had been knocked over, and the undead masses were surging against the invisible wall created by the glowing green flames. He continued moving through the courtyard, trampling the victims of Gorsbenor's insanity. As he heard bones crunch and flesh squish beneath his fists and feet, the living statue's face

189

contorted into a grimace of sheer sadness.

A stone tear fell from his left eye, and fell onto his chest, bouncing off and into the mass of dead.

As Benny looked outward beyond the perimeter of the courtyard, he saw his teammates ascending the path that wound upward on the adjoining hillside. The flame barricade flickered before his sight, and as he watched, first one then all five of the tripods were extinguished. The countless throng of undead flowed outward onto the road leading to the courtyard, then up the hill in pursuit of his compatriots.

"*NNNOOO!*" bellowed the living statue in a rage. He snarled, twisting his stone face into an expression of madness that he had never worn before. Benny quickened his stride, tossing the wooden bolt at several undead. Seeing a stone bench lying broken on its side, the statue bent down to retrieve it. He hefted the broken bench over his head and threw it into the running mass of undead. Screams and moans erupted from their dessicated throats as the stone tore into their bodies, ruining several.

Benny's stride turned into a trot, then a lope, and soon the rigid statue was actually running. He had never run before, and despite the harrowing situation, the feeling was exhilarating. He ran down the path after the tumbling and running bodies, then took the fork to run uphill after his friends. All the way, the statue was smashing into their pursuers. Yet, for each he knocked down, five took its place. And despite his pace, the scrambling, clawing, crawling and loping undead were faster in their mindless desperation. He could see them nearing his friends, and did his best to pick up his pace.

As he watched, Prince Corum, Tik-Tok, Captain Fyter,

and both great cats turned back to confront the horde of attackers. As they swung their weapons and did their best to fend off the undead, the statue's stone eyes turned upward and followed the retreat of General Jinjur and the others. A cluster of houses was assembled further up the hillside, and for the first time, Benny saw trees and rough shrubbery. The houses were darkened, likely abandoned, but the team was heading toward them. He recalled the boy Christian saying that his family resided in a house on a hill near the castle. Perhaps this was the boy's home.

Benny also thought of his teammate, Jo Files. The private from Oogaboo had spoken to him kindly, reminiscing about an adventure he had in a deserted castle with a gander named Benny. The same name was a coincidence, and a small source of amusement for both. Then Benny realized something else. These people were his friends, and he needed to rejoin them.

As more and more of the undead surged past the first line of defense, Benny saw his friend Private Files and Handy Mandy stop and wield their weapons. Thankfully the mountain path was narrow, and the undead were easily knocked down the hillside as much as the swords and spears slashed into them.

Benny's strides brought him close to the first line of attack, and he used his strength and weight to crush several undead from behind. The mindless creatures finally seemed to understand that the statue was a threat, and in futility tried to attack him as well.

The victims of their ruler's madness were incoherent and indistinguishable. Benny no longer saw faces, or even whether they had been male or female, young or old. All he saw was rotting flesh and scrabbling hands.

"About time you joined us, Public Benefactor!" shouted Prince Corum, using Benny's full name. The statue frowned, preferring his nickname, but said nothing. His fists were sweeping about, smashing into undead skulls and making a mess of those that they came into contact with.

The Cowardly Lion and Hungry Tiger both continued to roar and screech deafeningly, using their claws to rend the bodies of their attackers. Tik-Tok was spinning his upper torso, both arms outstretched. He managed to sever the bodies of every single undead that was foolish enough to get near him, and Captain Fyter was felling undead by droves with his musket in one hand and an axe in the other.

Piles of twitching bodies and ichor spread over the hillside, toppling downward from the path and littering the slope. The defensive line was holding well against the undead, but several of the creatures managed to surge past them. Higher up on the hill, Private Files and Handy Mandy were hacking away at those who managed to get past.

"How long will it take to stop them all?" gasped Corum. He placed his booted foot against the armless torso of an undead that he had run through with his sword, pushed back, and withdrew his darkened weapon from its ribcage. The yellow knight was splattered with ichor, but his eyes gleamed with something that had not shone in them for many a year. It appeared as if the former Sir Hokus of Pokes was enjoying himself. "No matter! Come, then! Have at thee!"

Gritting his stone teeth, the living statue joined his brethren in fending off the advancing horde. He hoped that whatever Zim and Maggie were capable of doing to get them out of there, that they would succeed. Soon.

Part 2
Chapter 10
What Lurks Beneath

THE SWAN CHARIOT landed in the center of the Emerald City, alighting at the foot of the grand staircase entry of Ozma's palace. To everyone's dismay, the people of the Emerald City looked haggard and sick. The few that had come out of their homes and businesses to greet their returning ruler were obviously miserable. Several held their stomachs, and others pressed their hands against their heads.

As Ak descended next to the chariot and let down his charges, the children, Herby, Glinda and the Master Woodsman looked about in bewilderment.

"Scraps? Scarecrow?" shrieked Dorothy, running up the steps.

"Return to me!" bellowed Ak, causing the Kansas girl to fall to her knees, scraping her shins on the emerald steps.

Glinda hefted up her gown and strode angrily up the steps with Ak and Herby. To Ozma and the children she spoke. "We will handle this."

Ozma helped Dorothy to rise. "We need to let them handle this," she said consolingly. Dorothy nodded, then sat down on a step, holding her hands over her shins.

"All right. But isn't there something we can do?"

"We don't even know what's going on," sighed Ozma, looking up at the three adults that were entering her palace. The sun was glinting off the emeralds that decorated every surface, and she wondered if there were any of the darkened sunglasses left from the days of old.

"Begging pardon," spoke up a voice from behind them. Dorothy and Ozma turned to see Button Bright, Trot and Betsy helping an old friend of theirs to walk over to the swan chariot. They assisted Jellia Jamb to sit on one of the chariot's benches, and looked imploringly at their ruler and the princess.

"Jellia!" cried Ozma, running over to her old friend. Dorothy, despite the pain in her shins, dashed with Ozma to kneel at Jellia's side. "What on earth happened here?"

The palace maid looked nervously up the steps. "E-everyone's sick, Ozma," she said. Her eyes drooped and she clutched at her stomach.

"Eat this," said Button Bright, shoving a sandwich toward her. Glinda had removed the food that they had taken from Burzee and stored it in a basket at their feet during their flight back.

"I'm not really hungry," said Jellia, smiling graciously despite her discomfort.

"You should eat this," insisted Ozma, taking the sandwich from the boy's hand and holding it out to Jellia. "It's from Burzee. It will make you better."

"All right," sighed the girl, accepting the leafy sandwich. She nibbled at the edges of it, swallowed, and smiled again.

"I suppose it might take a moment to work, right?"

The children nodded, encouraging Jellia and supporting her as she sat in the chariot.

The palace maid turned to Ozma. "Not moments after you left, everyone—every *flesh* person—in the palace starting getting sick. First Oscar, then me. All of the servants. Bob Up." She looked sadly at Dorothy. "Even Toto."

"What about the Jinjin?" asked the girl ruler. Surely the great Jinjin would never have allowed this to occur. "Where is he?"

"He left when you did. I suppose he had no reason to stay." Jellia coughed, then took another bite of the sandwich. "Perhaps he had business to attend to in his own land." She took an actual bite, chewed, and swallowed. "Oh," she said, her eyes relaxing somewhat. "This *is* good. Thank you."

Heartened by Jellia's speedy recovery, the children were even more astonished to look up and see a vast flock of flying creatures filling the air and landing throughout the Emerald City.

"Oh!" gasped Trot, clapping her hands and jumping up with joy. "Look!"

Fairies and ryls were flitting about the Emerald City, and they could see the fair folk clasping full satchels and boughs of berries.

"They've brought the cure!" exulted Betsy Bobbin, her smile nearly cutting her face in half. "Look! Everyone look!"

The swarm of benevolent beings were zooming in and out of homes and shops, and as they watched, the population of the Emerald City began to slowly stumble out of their buildings and into the sunlight.

Dorothy turned to face Jellia, a somber look upon her face once more. "But where are the Scarecrow and the others? What..."

"I don't know where they are," she added, turning an apologetic look to the princess. Jellia Jamb's face darkened as the color returned to her cheeks. She stood up in the chariot, her hands balled into fists. "The ghosts!" she said, scowling. "They did this! Klaus is in there." She pointed to Ozma's throne room. "And the others are with him!"

"The others?" repeated Ozma, casting a discouraged look at her old friend.

"Terrence and Christian," clarified Jellia. "They're with him."

Dorothy shook her head. "No," she said. "That can't be right. Terrence and Christian are *good*. I know it. I... I know it."

Ozma placed her hand tenderly on her old friend's shoulder. "Sometimes people can fool us," she said, sadly. "We will get to the bottom of this. We must trust Ak and Glinda."

"And Herby," added Button Bright. He thrust his hands into his pockets and walked a circle around the swan chariot, stepping over the reins.

"Zurline sent them," breathed Ozma with a smile. She waved at a group of fairies that were talking with some of the citizenry. "This is... this is very, *very* kind of them. But I would expect no less. They truly love us, don't they?"

"Definitely," laughed Betsy. "Come on! Why don't we see if we can help Glinda?" Without thinking, the girl dashed up the steps, followed by Trot. They ignored Ozma as she told them to wait, and were joined by Dorothy. Sighing, the girl ruler ran up the steps after her friends, leaving Jellia Jamb to keep the swans company.

"Well, I guess that leaves us," she said, turning to where she had seen Button Bright last. Blinking, Jellia realized that the boy was gone. Again.

• • •

As Glinda, Ak and Herby entered the great throne room of the Emerald City, what met their sights was a sad scene. Every wall of the throne room was lined with captives. Hanging from chains, dangling like marionettes, they saw the Scarecrow, the Patchwork Girl, the Tin Woodman, and even Bill, the metal rooster that had once served as a weathercock in the great outside world. Arranged among them were cages that contained their friends. Oscar Diggs and the Red Jinn lay in separate cages, with Toto, Eureka, Billina, Bob Up, Ojo, the Shaggy Man, and too many others to identify. They all moaned in agony, and to her horror Glinda saw Nox, the Keretarian Ox, hanging from several chains that were wrapped around his torso, neck, and belly.

"This ends! Here and now!" bellowed the thunderous voice of the Master Woodsman of the World. As Ak strode into the throne room, the chains holding up their people dissolved like smoke, letting the captives down gently to the floor. Cages opened, and those who could manage did their best to crawl out.

Rising from where he had been seated upon Ozma's throne, Klaus stood, facing the trio who had entered the scene of his conquest.

"Who dares oppose me?" spat the old wizard. "You think you can stop me? I was ancient before you were even born. You have no power, no hope to sway me. You are nothing to me!"

Klaus raised his hands, and a fiery sphere of energy formed above him. Lowering his hands to his front, the sphere launched at Ak, exploding in the Master Woodsman's face.

Ak stumbled backward, but remained on his feet. He took a deep breath through his nose. "Stay behind me, good Glinda. Herby. I will attend to this."

Folding his arms in front of him, Ak shook his head as if scolding a child. "You really believe that words can daunt me?" he asked, striding forward. His eyes took in the entire throne room, and he saw two other ghostly forms cowering behind the wizard. Using his uncanny powers of perception, Ak could see that Christian and Terrence were pure of soul, but they were greatly confused. Raising one hand before him, he flattened his hand sideways, and made a pushing motion with it. Klaus suddenly flew sideways, leaving Terrence and Christian to kneel at the base of the throne.

The wizard howled with rage and raised his arms for another volley of attack. Sighing, Ak deigned to glance sideways at him. He used the same hand, now turned downward, to make a brushing movement in Klaus' direction. The wizard, with a cry of dismay, went hurtling through the air and crashed through a window, sending shards of glass falling downward.

Thinking fast, Glinda muttered a hasty spell that caught the falling glass, and returned the shards to magically mend the broken window.

"How was he solid enough to break the glass?" wondered Herby. He had crouched down next to the Wizard of Oz, to whom he was feeding a Burzee sandwich, fortified with a handful of pills that he was passing out like candy.

"It was a trap," gasped Oscar Diggs, nearly choking on the food that Herby was pressing to his lips. He took a bite, swallowed it nearly whole, and rose to stand on wobbly legs. "We never saw it coming! He—"

The same window that Klaus had crashed out of once again shattered as the wizard flew back in, raging and crackling like lightning.

"You cannot stop *me!*" exulted the foreign wizard. His robes billowed about him like the ghost that everyone had accused him of being. A sphere of magical energy surrounded him, sending off sparks that danced like fire. "I am Necronimus! I am the slayer of fell beasts and ravager of worlds! All will come to know me as their doom! Kneel before me and witness your destruction!"

"Get. Out. Of. My. Home!"

Each word punctuated with a pause, Princess Ozma entered the throne room, leading behind her the three princesses. The girl ruler had her scepter raised high, extended outward from her. All of her frustration was focused into it, and a soft green glow burst forth, sending an arc toward the glowing sphere that Necronimus had swathed himself within.

The sphere turned green, and they could see Necronimus' face contort with rage and fury. Raising his own hands, Ak focused his own power to add to Ozma's. Jinnicky and Oscar Diggs rose to standing, leaning on each other. With what energy they could muster, they each raised their hands. There was no need for wands or any other magical tools. What innate magic they had inside flowed forth from them through their outstretched hands and joined the energy already surging from Ozma and Ak.

Necronimus resisted. His face, red with rage, was

turning black. The color of his skin steadily evolved from pink to grey to pitch, as if ink were flowing over him. The whites of his eyes burned red, and his beard turned to ash as his rage burned outward from within.

Ak, concentrating with all his might on sending the force of his goodness into the energy arc that resisted Necronimus' own, glanced again at Terrence and Christian. Tilting his head quickly, he gestured to Glinda, who followed his glance. The sorceress swiftly retrieved a thin wand from her sleeve and twirled it in their direction, moving it about in tiny circles. Once she had wound enough magic energy into it, she pulled it back toward herself, which in effect pulled the two ghosts to her. They slid across the floor, sweeping the shattered glass out of their paths and wound up at Glinda's feet. She pointed at the entrance behind her, through which the freed captives were fleeing, and into which a throng of fairies were coming.

The howl that broke from the necromancer's lips sent shivers down the spines of every living creature, whether flesh or not. As Glinda watched, the glowing sphere surrounding him began turning black, flickering against the combined magicks of Ozma, Oscar Diggs, Jinnicky and Ak. "Who is this man?" she whispered. There was no more time to evacuate the Ozians from the throne room. Raising her wand and her free hand, she brought both hands together in a clapping motion and forcibly expelled everyone—Dorothy, Trot, Betsy, Terrence, Christian, Scraps, the Scarecrow, Nox, Bill, Bob, and even the fairies of Burzee—in a mighty shove out of the throne room. The doors slammed shut behind them, and the magic onslaught against the evil wizard was joined by Glinda the Good.

"You forgot about me, dastard!" came a familiar voice from behind Necronimus. The evil one turned, his body arching hideously as he veritably burned from within. Queen Zixi of Ix ventured out of the Wizard's secret chamber behind the throne. Despite the mirrors that lined the walls, the witch queen of Ix braved encountering her reflection. Glinda could see an ancient crone reflected where the youthfully beautiful Zixi strode, her diaphanous gowns flaring about as the force of the magic created waves

that pressed against each of them. As Zixi raised her own hands to join with her allies, the reflected beldame in the mirrors straightened up. The old woman in the reflections, bent with age, grew taller and became a true reflection of the witch queen. "I will hide no longer."

Heartened, Glinda at last raised her wand, twirling it about to gather the magic about her and concentrate it into an arc which she shot at Necronimus. The energy coming from the sorceress was the red of love and strength, not the red of rage and terror that glowed in the evil wizard's eyes.

"I will not be stopped!" crowed the necromancer. His robes had burned away, leaving a blackened husk of a human being writhing in the burning sphere. "You can never contain me! I am the evil that burns in the hearts of every living creature. I am the secrets that hide behind your smiles and in the corner of your eyes. I am the whispers that travel through your veins, and the fear that grips your hearts. I am eternal!"

Ozma, tired, aggravated, frustrated, straining, and having recovered from sickness only to find this trouble in her home, said the only thing that came to her mind. "Oh, do shut up!"

Smirking, Glinda drew strength from her friend's comment. It was so very amusing that the good sorceress could not help but let forth a burst of laughter.

Zixi, glancing at the other good witch, tilted her head. Seeing Glinda laugh brought a smile to her face, and she, too, let a snicker slip from her lips. Her giggle became a chuckle, and it turned into a laugh, and then a guffaw.

Ak, the Wizard of Oz and the Red Jinn caught the wave of mirth and began laughing.

"She told you to shut up! Har har har! What a riot, eh, Wiz? She said 'shut up'! Ha ha ha!" The Red Jin nearly fell over, laughing so heartily that his jar rattled about himself. "Shut up! Ha ha ha! Shut up! Har har har! Hee hee hee!"

Sobering, Glinda added, "Indeed. Do shut up." She considered the evil one's words, knowing full well that there were dark times in her past when she was guilty of making choices that might not be considered benevolent. Her protégé, standing only paces from her and lending his magic to the effort, was guilty of kidnapping their very ruler when she was a baby, and handing her over to Mombi. Yet there he stood, defending her with all his might. Glinda, smiling, nodded to herself. She reached into a pocket in her gown and retrieved a small glass bottle. It was stoppered with a cork, and the body of it was thick red glass. With her thumbnail she popped the cork off, catching it quickly and holding it in her palm while she grasped the neck of the bottle. With a sigh, she poured the contents of the bottle out, knowing that its contents would be wasted. No sacrifice. More could be made later.

"Ozma said for him to shut up," she said loud enough to be heard over the crackle of magic and the screeching of the necromancer. "Good advice." She held up the bottle so all could see. As their laughter died down, each magic user focused their energy on the bottle, forcing Necronimus toward the sorceress of the south and her outstretched hand.

"Never! You will never contain me! I am the filth that covers your eyes when you are blind! I am the pricking of your thumbs as something wicked comes! Each tear that burns with rage! Each scream that burns your lungs. I am the—"

As the sphere was pushed toward Glinda, she raised the bottle to touch it to the glowing, crackling orb. Her hand shook with the effort, but as contact was made, all gathered heard a loud sucking noise, then a slurp, and then a pop as the sphere, with Necronimus in it, was instantly drawn into the bottle. Glinda dropped her wand and stopped the bottle with the cork.

"Not done yet," she muttered, pulling a spool of cord from another pocket in her gown. The spool sparkled pink and white, and she wound the string first over, then around the lid of the bottle, and continued winding it around the entirety of the bottle.

"May I?" asked Zixi, reaching out for the bottle. As Glinda handed it over to their ally from across the desert, she saw Zixi's reflection once again was that of an ancient, haggard old woman. In respect for their friend, and with a wave of her hand, Glinda caused all the mirrors in the throne room to cloud over.

Queen Zixi grasped the red bottle in her right hand, and with her wand clasped in her left, she spoke the words of a spell.

"Sands of time, from near and far
Come now, hear me, travel near
I command you, gather 'round
And bind this bottle, bind it here."

As she spoke, a cloud of sand streamed in from the shattered window, refining itself to the thickness of the same twine that Glinda had wrapped around the bottle. The sand coalesced around the bottle, wrapping it in a cocoon of fine grains of stone until the red was gone and Zixi grasped a solidified mass of sand.

Ak reached out for the bottle, and Zixi willingly gave

it to him. "I have heard tell that the Red Jinn of Ev can command the fires of the ruby," he said, holding the coated bottle in front of him. "Is this true?"

"Oh? Oh! Yes. Yes indeedy! Har har! Yes! Good idea!" The diminutive wizard turned to his rival and friend, Oscar Diggs. "I could use a hand. Not quite up to snuff, you know. Join me?"

"Of course, my friend," replied the Wizard of Oz, bowing politely to the Red Jinn.

"Let's come up with a rhyme, shall we?" Jinnicky twisted his face comically, pressing his fingers to his lips. "What'll it be...? Something with rubies and emeralds and fire and such..."

"There's no need for that," commented the Wizard. "Let's just burn it solid." He looked at Ak. "It won't hurt you, will it?"

The Master Woodsman of the world laughed. "No indeed! Have at it, my friends. I shall not let it drop. Do not worry."

With twin smiles, the wizards pointed their wands at the sand-encrusted bottle. "Let's at least say 'abra cadabra,' eh?" suggested Oscar to the Jinn, who nodded emphatically.

"Abra cadabra!" they both shouted in unison, sending a burst of red and green energy at the bottle, which commingled white and sealed the sand to solid.

With a smile, Ak nodded approvingly. "I shall take this bottle to where it will be forgotten for all eternity. Your assistance is greatly appreciated. The fairies will take care of the sick. This foolishness is over and done with." He nodded at his friends, and nonchalantly walked to the doorway. Pushing the doors open with a free hand, Ak departed without a backward glance.

Part 2
Chapter u
Loving Arms

JAYNE was a plain girl, though she was only so because of the rags she wore, and the dirt that practically coated her from head to foot. It was fortunate that Zim and Maggie entered the hovel before any of the others did, for they were able to see straightaway that the girl was alive, and not undead. She was the only living soul in the cluster of houses.

"Christian promised me he would return. He promised that, just like our parents promised. And they have not come back." The girl cried unashamedly, burying her face in Maggie's arms. "I've been waiting…"

For her part, the good witch could do little to remedy the situation. Her old bones were beginning to ache, and she could distinctly feel the cold. Rheumatism was scraping against her joints, and even her jaw ached. She gazed tired eyes at her husband, who smiled reassuringly at her.

It seemed that for this entire expedition, Maggie found herself either assisting or being assisted. And that was fine with her. She was too old to be at the forefront. Her job was to heal and mend, and comforting the distraught child in her arms was the most important work she had done thus far.

"Your brother is back in Oz, where we came from," she said after the girl's sobs had subsided into sniffles. "We came here to find you. Is there anyone else left here?"

Jayne shook her head, her lips quivering. "I've been... it's... it's... it's just me. Just me. All alone."

Maggie wanted to ask Jayne just how long she had been alone, but she realized that the "ghosts" had been in the Emerald City for nearly two years, and that Christian spoke of his parents having gone missing before that. The witch looked up and around, hoping to see food stores in the tiny hut. Seeing none, she hugged the little girl close, feeling her ribs stick out against her sides.

"Zim," she said to her husband. "She could use some food. What have we brought?"

The tall sorcerer was standing at the entrance of the hovel, watching the melee as their friends fought off the undead down on the hillside. He turned his back to the door and knelt down next to his wife. The satchel that she had been carrying for him was lying at their feet, and he reached into it, pulling out two jars and a paper bag.

Zim spoke. "Cream of mushroom soup, fruit tea, and cheese sandwiches." Smiling, the slender man opened the lids of the jars and removed the sandwiches from the bag. "What a splendid idea. Let's eat." He sat down cross-legged next to Maggie, and doled out the three sandwiches that were in the bag. Reaching into the satchel, he pulled out three small bowls and three teacups, into which he portioned out just enough soup and tea for each of them.

"Of course we must remember to wash our hands, first," suggested Maggie as she accepted a moist napkin from her husband. She wiped her hands with it, and handed another to the little girl. Jayne followed Maggie's example.

The sounds of battle echoed upward to them where they sat, but the Greenleafs chose to focus on Jayne and enjoyed the small meal with her.

For her part, the girl tore into the food. As she drained her cup and bowl, Zim thoughtfully refilled them from the seemingly bottomless jars.

As they ate, they were surprised to see Handy Mandy looking into the hut. "There you are!" she said, wiping sweat and filth from her face with some of her free hands. She still wielded two swords and a spear, as well as her shield, but the girl seemed calm, and almost hopeful.

"We're winning," she said to Zim and Maggie, eyeing the food. It was then that she noticed the girl in Maggie's lap. "Oh! Hello!" Hastily, Mandy sheathed the rest of her weapons, leaning the spear and shield against the wall as she entered.

Wearing an American military uniform with a helmet, covered with ichor and blood, Handy Mandy presented a terrifying sight with her seven arms extended toward the girl. It was the genuine kindness behind the smile on her face that told Jayne that this was a good person. Zim and Maggie were neither as soiled as Mandy was.

Zim extended a squeeze-bottle to Mandy and directed her to spread a drop of its contents over her hands. *Hamamelis* to disinfect your hands," he explained. He then reached into the paper sack and withdrew two more sandwiches. He handed them to Mandy, who tore into them greedily, then filled a mug with tea for her.

"Our forces?" he asked, wanting to know how they fared.

Mandy swallowed, smiling. "Not bad!" she said, laughing and nearly choking on the food. She took a swallow of tea, then sat down next to them on the floor. "I mean, we're not doing too bad. Corum and Benny and the Lion and the Tiger are taking care of most of them. Fyter too." Mandy looked over her shoulder as she ate, noticing that the sky outside was lightening. "The sun will rise soon," she said, turning back to her friends. She smiled once again at the little girl, who smiled shyly back at her. "This dark night might finally be over."

Prophetic words, thought the flying sorcerer as he finished his tea. "Just leave the dishes here," he said to the others. "We might have use for them later. Or not."

Once again they were joined by one of their fellow Ozians. Tik-Tok, hearing their voices, stumbled on wobbly feet into the hut. "Wind me up," he spoke, mechanically. "Wind me up. Wind me up."

Mandy jumped up, her seven arms spread out like a spider. Clearly Tik-Tok's thinking had almost completely wound down, and his movement was getting dangerously close to stopping. With a few twists, Mandy had the clockwork man wound back up again tightly. He bowed, doffing his hat, and stood straight up again. "My grat-i-tude, Man-dy," he said, punctuating each syllable. "Hel-lo," he said to the little girl seated on Maggie's lap.

"This is Tik-Tok," said Maggie to Jayne. "He's a friend, too. Just like Mandy." To the clockwork man, she asked, "Is it... is it almost... done? Out there?"

"There are a few rem-nants," replied the copper man. "But nev-ver fear. We shall soon o-ver-come them. It is just a mat-ter of time." To Mandy, he added, "Your as-sis-tance is need-ed. I will re-main here."

Wordless, Mandy arose and cast an apologetic look at Zim, Maggie and Jayne. She waved all seven of her hands at the little girl, smiling encouragingly.

Maggie smiled back at the goat girl, and spoke. "We'll see her again. You will see *all* of the friends who came with us. But for now, let's just stay here where it's safe. Tell me, where have you been sleeping?"

Jayne lifted herself off of Maggie's lap and grasped the elderly woman's hand. Maggie arose and followed the little girl to a corner of the hovel, where a stove and a pile of wood obstructed the corner. Behind them, Maggie saw a nest of blankets where the little girl had been hiding for some time. Frowning sadly, Maggie saw how dirty and thin the blankets were.

"You are coming back with us," she said quietly, tightening her grip on Jayne's hand. To Zim, she added, "and that's final."

• • •

The battle on the hillside was subsiding, but Corum, Fyter, the great cats, and Jinjur continued to hack away at undead that came mindlessly after them. Benny had slowed down to almost a standstill, remaining virtually motionless on the hillside. Jo Files and Notta were trudging about wearily, doing their best to avoid undead that were crawling and dragging broken bodies. Kak and Stampedro continued to whack away at the undead that they encountered. The horse's hooves smashed bones and skulls, leaving a trail of filth and desiccation.

The powerful horse stamped about angrily, kicking tiredly but adamantly. Ahead of him, Stampedro saw Kak lift a rock nearly as big as his own head and smash it down on one of the undead that was dragging itself toward the battle. The monkey's eyes were glassed over, and he could see despair painted over the simian's face. Shaking his mane, Stampedro did his best to put such thoughts from his own mind.

Two undead people were stumbling toward Stampedro from below on the hillside. Both of them looked as if they had been recently killed. The larger of the two wore a chef's cap, and half of his head had been caved in as if something heavy had been smashed into it. The horse's spirit nearly fell. There seemed to be no end to the swarm of Gorsbenor's victims. Turning his back to them, the horse prepared to kick back with his heels, certain to smash them to pieces.

"Enough!" cried a voice that none of them expected to hear. A brilliant flash of green light flooded the hillside, competing with the sunrise, and from within the blinding glare stepped a familiar figure. She was dressed in her regal gown with her curly brown hair billowing back from the dainty crown and two poppies fastened on either side of her head. The gentle face of Ozma looked out upon the field of carnage, and tears began to stream from her eyes. "No more! Stop! *Stop!*"

Stampedro willingly obliged, ignoring the two dead creatures that were slowly ambling toward him.

The girl ruler could no longer remain behind, knowing that her people were engaging in willful acts of violence. It did not matter that they did that in a proactive stance to subert evil. The fact remained that her people were doing it, and she was responsible for them. It was time for her to put an end to it.

From their positions on the hillside, the rest of the team looked to where Ozma had appeared, and cries of joy and hope resounded from each of them. They did not see the pain and sorrow painted upon her face, or they would not have celebrated so happily.

"Zim Greenleaf!" shouted Ozma at the top of her lungs.

Hearing his name, the green sorcerer immediately leapt to his feet. Casting a harried glance at his wife, Tik-Tok and Jayne, he sped from the hovel and dashed down the hillside to where he'd heard Ozma's voice come from.

Unlike the others, Zim felt great trepidation upon seeing his ruler there in the hills of Flora. She was like a beam of sunlight breaking through dark storm clouds. The sun was climbing up into the sky, illuminating the carnage that littered the entire area. As far as the eye could see, the bodies of the undead lay either motionless or writhing, spilling blood and ichor and moaning pitiably.

Zim slowed to a jog as he neared Ozma, then fell to his knees to bow before her. He looked up to meet her gaze.

An expression of anger and pain contorted Ozma's face. Her lips were bared back, exposing her clenched teeth as her forehead was furrowed in concern. She was clearly upset, and seeing the hillside covered with moaning undead—severed limbs moving about, bodies cut in half and dragging themselves along the hillside, flesh falling off and organs falling out—traumatized her. These were victims of madness and evil to the extreme.

"Ozma—we... they... are not killing live people. We are demolishing empty, soulless corpses animated by evil magic. Their souls are gone—have gone to wherever souls go. I hope the souls of these people are happier now— wherever they are."

Ozma regarded the exceptionally tall man as he kneeled before her. She took his words into consideration, but her anger was not lessened. "Make this right," she said through gritted teeth. Then, softening upon seeing the great sorrow upon Zim's face and those of her friends, she added, "How can I help?"

• • •

"He already knew what to do, didn't he?" asked Mandy. She returned to retrieve Maggie and Jayne from the hut on the hillside. The little girl had fallen asleep in the old witch's arms, and despite her exhaustion, Maggie refused to relinquish the child to Mandy.

The goat girl from Mount Mern grasped her white cap in one hand, and still held tight to all her weapons with her other hands. She drew close to where Maggie stood, overlooking the hillside below them. Prince Corum and Captain Fyter were still hacking away at some of the undead that still came at them, but for the most part the zombies either lay motionless or had been rendered too damaged to put up any more fight.

Mandy and Maggie regarded Zim and Ozma, positioned downhill from the huts, but above most of the carnage. As they watched, Zim unbuttoned his coat, reached into his vest and removed a small pouch that was bound around his waist. From within he removed a tendril of Ozma's pothos plant. It was brown, thick and dry, the leaves stripped from most of its length with only a small wilted leaf on the end. Though Mandy and Maggie could not see it, Ozma recognized the plant, having seen it spreading so abundantly in her own throne room.

"Yes," answered Maggie quietly, rocking the girl gently in her arms. She knew that Zim had hoped against hope that Gorsbenor's victims could be helped, and the damage reversed. Sighing at the futility of it, she took hope in her spouse's ability. "Watch."

The witch's husband raised the pothos tendril above himself, holding it as if it were a magic wand. He cast a silent look at his wife, who beamed back her smile. Zim looked to Ozma, who placed her hand in his free hand. The sorcerer began chanting incoherently under his breath.

The tendril began to move. As Mandy, Maggie, and all the others watched, it grew more supple and green. Small buds began to appear on its length, and soon leaves began to grow from them. The tendril lengthened, sending out more tendrils which extended down to the rocky ground. Zim tenderly set the pothos in an area where some soil was exposed between crags. Instantly the plant sent roots down into it. The plant's force was so strong that its roots began chipping and cracking the larger rocks at their feet.

Before their very eyes, and at an unbelievable speed, pothos tendrils began racing down the hillside. Each shoot sent roots downward, engendering more tendrils to spread outward in a web, cracking into the stone face of the mountainside. Soon, the hillside below them was green with vibrant leaves. As the plants approached the undead, they wrapped their tendrils about appendages and then *into* them. Each of the undead stopped moving instantly as the plants overtook them, and soon blessed silence relieved them all.

It took only ten minutes for every single undead to be ensnared by the tenacious pothos plant. Corum, Captain Fyter, and all the other members of the team watched in awe and confusion as Zim and Ozma continued their work on the hillside.

"It was a trap. Gorsbenor is dead. The charms didn't work," explained the sorcerer to Ozma as they watched the plants cover more and more of the hillside. He looked down at his feet, feeling as if he had betrayed the girl ruler.

Ozma smiled encouragingly at him. "It was Necronimus. He erased the portal from the doorway. None of us saw it coming. We were far too trusting." Seeing Zim's alarmed reaction, she continued. "He has been subdued. Christian and Terrence are in the Emerald City. Tollydiggle is having them stay with her until we get this sorted out. It's for the best."

Zim nodded. Speaking again, he added, "There is... no hope for the people here." He shrugged his shoulders, closing his eyes in resignation. Zim sighed, "I cannot resurrect the dead—much as I would like to."

"I know."

He wondered what triggered the undead to attack when they did, but chose not to inquire. The time for that would come later, when a thorough investigation could be conducted.

As the sun filled the sky over castle Flora, the combatants found themselves knee-deep in verdant leaves that rustled gently in the morning breeze. From far off came the smell of ocean, which helped to wipe away any lingering traces of the fell horror that they had fought off.

Zim once again reached into the pouch and withdrew a handful of seeds. "*Cynodon dactylon*. It spreads and covers, and converts organic matter to mulch by creating a thick cover under which..."

Ozma held up her hand. "I don't need to know how it works. Bermuda grass, correct?"

"Indeed. Also, *fragaria x ananassa*. Spreading, fragrant, nutritious. Strawberries. *Ficus carica*—fig. It normally thrives on flat lands, but this variety is hearty enough to grow anywhere. And *cucumis sativus*. Spreading cucumbers."

"Sounds wonderful, Zim. Please go on."

Zim smiled smugly, losing himself in his pride and joy. "Lastly, *musa x paradisiacal gillikinus*. It's a special hybrid that I cultivated in the Gillikin highlands: mountain-hardy banana trees. And this is the perfect place to try them out."

Ozma nodded in appreciation of the wizard's prowess.

The botanist cupped the seeds in the palm of his hand, and held them to his lips. He blew the seeds outward, and they watched as the morning wind carried the strawberry, fig, banana, and Bermuda grass seeds far and wide.

Far below them, the pothos tendrils were wending upward again toward castle Flora.

Ozma asked, "Will they overtake the castle?"

"Yes. The entire land will return to the green. Perhaps some years hence people will once again make their home here. They will discover a plentitude of strawberries, cucumbers, bananas, and figs." The sorcerer gazed about his handiwork, smiling as he noticed new leaves sprouting upward from underneath the pothos vines. His charmed seeds were taking root, and soon the entire mountainside and valley would be unrecognizable.

"You've taken it upon yourself to make that choice, then?" asked Ozma, still watching the vines crawl over the castle.

"Choice, your majesty?" asked Zim, taken aback. His voice cracked with uncertainty. "What do you mean?"

"Choice," echoed Ozma.

The flying sorcerer considered his queen's words. Sighing, he blinked in resignation. "Yes, I've chosen to have the plants eradicate the castle and all signs of civilization. What happened here was too dark, too evil, too horrible for history to bear witness to." He gulped, daring to look at Ozma. The fairy ruler of Oz kept her eyes trained on the castle. Green traveled up the sides and throughout the heart of the grey stone structure.

Ozma breathed deeply, inhaling the fragrance of the white strawberry blossoms that poked through patches of grass, vines, and bourgeoning tree trunks. Growth that eventually quelled the movement of the lingering undead that they covered. "All right," she said. She turned to him and smiled. "Let's go home, shall we?"

• • •

Tommy Kwikstep looked up at the towering mass of undead flesh as the winding tendrils of the plants creeped downward to where he, Perry, and the creature lay. He was too exhausted to even pick up the sword that he had so desperately used to fight off the terrifying aberration.

As he closed his eyes, he replayed his actions, marveling how he had found the strength to defeat the thing.

Perry was relying on him. Perry, who now lay motionless in his arms, counted on him for protection. Tommy had wielded the sword with the skill of desperation, hacking off the creature's arms, driving it into the creature's chest, and hacking away at its head until he was able to sever it, all the while bleeding profusely from the bone fragments embedded in his body.

As the creature fell, and the chains bounced against the foundation walls of the castle, Tommy had made his way back to Perry. Neither of them could move any further, but as worn out as he was, Tommy would not allow sleep to overcome him. It took all his strength to pull his old hat out of his satchel and put it on.

"Stay awake, Perry. Please. Don't close your eyes."

And now Perry was unmoving. Tommy, his face streaked with blood and tears, could only watch as the plants consumed the remains of the creature he had fought off, then climb up the castle walls. The plant tenderly brushed against him and Perry as it grew, but unlike the creature, which it consumed, the plant left both young men untouched.

As the sun rose, Tommy smiled, knowing that victory was theirs. This was the work of Zim Greenleaf. Closing his eyes, Tommy relaxed his tensed body, and leaned down to lie on the bed of supple leaves.

"Not yet," came a voice, and his eyes opened to see Ozma and Zim standing before them, with the Hungry Tiger and Benny behind them. The last thing he felt before losing consciousness was being lifted in the strong arms of the living statue.

Part 2
Chapter 12
The Investigation

AS ZIM EXPECTED, a thorough investigation was carried out to determine what exactly occurred while various parties were absent from the Emerald City. Ozma wanted to know *how* Necronimus did what he did, and when he did it. The *why* was obvious. He was a bad man, and an exceptionally powerful wizard. But the ramifications of the events would be deeper felt.

"We were too trusting," explained the girl ruler to the group that she called together in the council chamber.

• • •

General Jinjur was beside herself. "My son! My son!" Her screams were high pitched and frenzied, and she clawed at her own face in agony when Corum and Files were tasked to hold her back. Zim and Maggie carefully removed bone shards from both young men's bodies, and then spread poultices and powders over their gaping wounds before carefully bandaging them up.

As torn and bloodied clothes were handed back to

Kak, who flew them off and tossed them into the valley below, General Jinjur was reduced to mindless sobbing, wailing, and pulling at her own hair. She had thrown her helmet down the hillside, and was tearing at the buttons of her jacket in frustration. Seeing the stalwart general so demeaned and downtrodden was more than many of them could tolerate, and tears were shed all around. Handy Mandy, whom Maggie finally allowed to hold Jayne, did her best to shield the child from the sights of triage, and walked with her up the hillside a bit. The child was so malnourished that she barely weighed a thing. They found some fig trees that already were laden with ripe fruit, and she showed her how to pick and eat them.

Getting back from Flora to Oz was a simple matter, once Oscar Diggs, Zixi, and the Red Jinn restored the portal in the Wizard's chamber behind the throne. After Zim and Maggie had done their best to treat Tommy and Perry, and Handy Mandy handed Jayne back to the old woman, Mandy was the first to try the return charm again. Seeing the seven-armed girl disappear was all the team needed. Sending their injured through first, within moments, each of them did their own part to return to Oz.

Zim, Maggie, Jayne and Ozma were left to take one swift look at the kingdom of Flora, now aptly named. Thick-leaved fig trees were scattered across the mountainside, and already birds were curiously flying in from far off lands, attracted by the strong scent of the ripened fruit. With satisfaction, Zim saw insects flitting about the strawberries and cucumbers. Any sign of movement from the undead were completely subjugated by roots and vines that would turn them into mulch in the course of time. The arboreal plants—banana and fig—already welcomed brave birds.

"Life returns," he said with gratitude. There was no telling where the insects had come from. He looked down at his blood-stained clothes, and sighed. "But we have wounded to attend to."

"Pretty," murmured Jayne, her arms wrapped about Maggie's neck. The trauma that she had gone through would be dealt with once they returned home. Maggie already knew how she was going to handle things, and she resolutely knew that her husband would just have to accept matters.

Clasping hands with Ozma, Zim and Maggie repeated the words of the spell together, and in the twinkling of an eye, the four of them were gone.

• • •

Zim's healing magic had Tommy Kwikstep and Perry on the mend. Perry and Tommy needed powerful antibiotics to stave off any potential infections they might have gotten from being pierced by the bones of dead people. With Herby's capable assistance, both healers had sequestered the couple and allowed no one to near them—not even General Jinjur—until they were certain that their healing charms and medicines were effective.

The investigation was to be headed by the Great Jinjin, who was asked to return even though he had recently departed for his own realm. There would likely be no one as impartial as he, and this was a matter of importance not only for the security of Ozma and her people, but in the matter of ethics as well. Ozma had to come to terms with the fact that she herself was the one who instigated the invasion; despite pulling back and regretting her choice. The council she organized went ahead with the effort, and for that she knew she was responsible. Ozma recused herself from the investigation, admitting her own role in the matter. She blamed no one else.

It was determined that Necronimus had set the trap long before anyone knew of him, Terrence, or Christian. The wizard had sought out a victim to further his goal, and despite Gorsbenor's dastardliness, the prince regent was merely a tool. Befriending Terrence and Christian was also part of the wizard's scheme, and it worked smoothly enough to get the prince to travel to Oz, bring Ozians back, and allow enough magical energy to transfer between realms to pull the necromancer into it. His own dark magic was such that Lurline's enchantment prevented him from coming in on his own. He had to be in the company of people who belonged in Oz. Thus, bringing four children to Flora guaranteed that he could "piggyback" a ride with them upon their return.

Making the children and Ozma sick took time; the enchantments upon Oz did not easily allow illness into its realm, but over time and with great efforts, the dark magic he kept to himself infected them. Although it only made them ill and failed to incapacitate them entirely as he'd hoped, still, it was an unforeseen benefit to have them depart for Glinda's palace and then Burzee at the most opportune time. That gave the wizard the opportunity to attack and take over the Emerald City virtually unopposed. From there, he easily erased the return portal so that the team of liberators could not return, but not before sending through a command for the undead to attack.

The disposal of the conquered villain was taken care of by Ak. Though his final fate was unknown, at least they knew Ak could be trusted to ensure he would never pose a threat again.

The actions of Jinjur, Zim, Corum, Handy Mandy, Benny, Captain Fyter, Jo Files, Notta Bit More, Kak, Tommy Kwikstep, Perry, Stampedro, and Maggie were something that Ozma felt she needed to address. Tik-Tok was deemed blameless, for he was a machine that only did as he was told. Ozma blamed herself for not ordering him to stand down. As she felt herself guilty for having instigated the team and planted the idea of liberation in their minds, Ozma could not find it in herself to punish them. For Jinjur's zealousness, Ozma could only find her guilty of doing what came naturally to her. How could she fault someone for doing what they knew to do?

In the end, Ozma decided to abolish and absolve the investigation's findings on her people. Their own consciences would weigh their actions, and she knew that the good people of Oz were not likely proud of what they had done. Ozma owed them apologies and reparations, especially to Perry and Tommy.

"And that is why we are here, in the royal gardens, where this all began," she said, speaking to the group of people gathered closely about her. Among them were Christian and Terrence. "This is the Fountain of Oblivion.

"Once before, when the crew of the *Crescent Moon* came home after experiencing perhaps the most dreadful experience of their lives—not in the extreme that you all have, but something just as bad—I gave them the option to drink from the fountain. Most of them declined, and they live with their memories. Those memories have shaped them and influenced them, but they are all good people."

Ozma gestured at the sign mounted on a silver stake in front of the fountain. ALL PERSONS ARE FORBIDDEN TO DRINK AT THIS FOUNTAIN. "There is a reason for that sign. I control who drinks from this fountain. Once, many years ago, a little girl used some of its water to..." Ozma felt at the poppies on her crown, remembering her adventures with Lambert and Toby after she had unknowingly drank of the fountain's waters. She shook her head. "Never mind that," she said.

"I give you the same option that I gave to the crew of the *Crescent Moon*. If you choose to drink from this fountain, the events that you experienced in Flora will be wiped from you. Breathe in the mist and you will lose only a day. One drop will erase a year. One cup and you will lose years." She looked at Christian and Terrence as she spoke the last sentence, her gaze penetrating their semi-transparent forms. "You could start over, completely."

Handy Mandy needed no time to make her decision. She took a deep breath, strode forward to stand at the edge of the fountain, and leaned over. Inhaling deeply, the goat girl from Mount Mern turned back to look at her friends. "Why, hello! What are we all doing here?" She laughed merrily, then quieted when she saw the somber faces around her. "Has... has something happened?"

Ozma reached out a hand to one of Mandy's seven. "It's all right dear. Nothing that we will bother you with. Nox is waiting for you. A terrible villain tried to take over the Emerald City, and he was tied up. I'm sure he wants to tell you all about it!"

"Oh, my! Oh goodness! Excuse me!" The seven-armed girl ran as fast as her wooden-clogged feet would let her, which was surprisingly fast. Her departure fortified the others' confidence in the power of the fountain.

"I will," volunteered Notta Bit More, the circus clown. "This was never something for a clown." He removed his red rubber nose, leaned over the rim of the fountain, and breathed in the mist. "Ah!" he said, a broad grin spreading across his face.

The others, knowing how to act from seeing Mandy's reaction, all smiled and applauded as the clown turned a somersault and laughed gleefully at them. "What's the to-do? What's the hubbub, bubs? Where's Bob?"

Ozma told the clown the same that she had told Mandy, and soon the bewildered circus performer was running off, his oversized shoes slapping against the cobblestone path of the garden.

Of the others who had traveled to Flora, none stepped forward. Stampedro nickered and blew his breath from his nostrils, but the remainder of the team kept their tongues. Kak even went so far as to leap up and take flight, landing in the branches of a nearby tree in the garden. The Cowardly Lion hesitantly crept forward, then backed away, shaking his great maned head. Tommy and Perry, both covered with bandages from head to toe, stood arm in arm, steadfast and unmoving.

"I will not forget that we have a little girl waiting for us to take care of her," informed Maggie Greenleaf. She linked her arm through Zim's, who nodded in agreement. "May we have your leave, your majesty?"

Ozma nodded. The witch and the wizard turned, smiled at their friends, and departed the private garden.

Kak was not so polite, and scampered through the branches of the tree to disappear from their sight.

Shoulders drooped, the rest of the team filtered away, leaving General Jinjur, Benny, Terrence and Christian to face Ozma alone. The general cast a sorrowful look as her son and his partner limped painfully. She realized that they

would heal, but wondered if the emotional scars would be deeper.

"It was a..." Jinjur fumbled for the right words. "It was a tactical decision. We were led into a trap. I did the best that I could to lead our people to safety and return home. In the end, we defended ourselves. Never once did we attack anyone." She pressed her lips tightly together, doing her best to maintain her composure, but Ozma could see tears welling up in the general's eyes. This was a woman accustomed to the idea of war, but having lived in Oz so long, had no real concept of what that meant, of the price that war demands. The possibility of her own son suffering—and almost dying—had given her pause to reconsider the stance Ozma had long taken against violence. "I... I thought you were soft. I thought I was right... I..." Tears streamed freely down Jinjur's face.

"I know," said Ozma softly. She smiled sadly at the general. "Thank you for coming today, my friend. Go tend to your son."

Jinjur bowed deeply, then snapped erect, saluting Ozma. She clicked her heels together, turned abruptly, and marched off.

ALL PERSONS ARE
FORBIDDEN TO DRINK
AT THIS FOUNTAIN

Ozma turned her gaze to the living statue, who had remained silent for the duration.

"I cannot drink," said Benny sadly. The breath left Ozma's lungs and she did her best not to cry out. Seeing the stone man so visibly upset cut to her soul and the queen of Oz could do nothing but look pityingly at him. Tears cascaded down Ozma's cheeks as the living statue stared sadly downward.

"I'm sorry, Benny," she said. "That's my fault. I'm *so* sorry."

"Our actions were, in a sense, a favor to Necronimus's victims, who would not want their reanimated corpses used for evil ends. You, and by extension, the army you put together, helped put them to rest, saved the life of a young girl, and prevented further evil from occurring." The living statue smiled encouragingly at Ozma, bowed his head, turned slowly, and lumbered off, exiting the secret garden.

Ozma's eyes remained closed, her mind processing everything that was going on. Benny's desire to drink from the fountain—and his inability to—cut her deepest, and her sorrow burned terribly. His words comforted her, but she still felt great anguish for all that had occurred.

The girl ruler heard hands reach into the water, and opened her eyes to see Terrence and Christian sitting on the edge of the fountain, cupping a handful of water each.

"They called us ghosts," said Terrence darkly, staring moodily ahead of him, but looking at nothing. He breathed in deeply. "I want to be a ghost." He looked at Ozma. "I want to be a ghost," he repeated. And before Ozma could stop him, he lifted his hands to his lips and drank every drop of the water.

Ozma's jaw dropped and she could only watch in horror as Christian mimicked his friend's action. With a sigh of relief, she saw that the boy let the water splash back into the fountain.

Terrence nodded kindly at Christian, but said nothing. Despite having his memory wiped, there appeared to be a lingering sadness about him.

Christian, for his part, smiled broadly back at Terrence. He thrust out his hand. "Hello. Do you know who I am?"

Terrence shook his head and smiled in confusion. "I'm... not sure. I guess I don't know." He looked in wonderment at the lovely garden around them, then saw Ozma standing close by them. She had recovered herself, and smiled in welcome at them. With amusement, she realized that their speech patterns no longer seemed antiquated. Perhaps they had absorbed enough vernacular to affect their new lives. Leaves rustled behind them, and Ozma spied the winged monkey Kak hiding in the brush. She smiled reassuringly at the young simian.

"My name is Ozma. This is my private garden. You are in the Emerald City, and you are—" She choked on the word, but managed to speak after a pause. With an encouraging nod from Christian, who chose at the last second to retain his memories, she spoke. "You are ghosts. You haunt my castle, and that's perfectly normal. You are welcome here, and you have many, many friends. Your name is Terrence." She waved toward the towers of her palace above the greenery. "Would you like to see the rest of the palace? You even have your own rooms in the castle. It's all quite lovely and wonderful."

Ozma led Terrence and Christian from the secret garden. As they passed the garden gate, she closed it and locked it behind them. Standing in the garden proper were Zim, Maggie, Benny, Button Bright, and Jo Files. Movement in the branches above them told Ozma that Kak was still lingering about. As luck would have it, Button Bright chose that moment to appear, having "lost" himself in the Emerald City once they returned from Burzee. Maggie held Jayne in her arms. The little girl was dressed in clean new clothes, and beamed a smile at Christian upon seeing him walk up with Ozma.

"Hi Christian!" she said happily. Maggie let her down, and the girl hugged her brother tentatively, confused by his diaphanous appearance. Jayne was clearly taller than Christian, having aged in the two years she was alone in Flora. "I can see through you! Are... are you a ghost?"

"Yes," said the boy, happy to see her familiar face. "I suppose I am."

"I'm going to stay with Maggie and Zim a little while," she explained. "Will you come with us? Or will you stay here?" She was still puzzled at his appearing her age, despite her relief at seeing him.

Maggie smiled somewhat sadly. "I think he's going to stay here for a little while," she said softly. "But we will visit often." She looked insightfully at Ozma, realizing that focusing on helping Jayne adjust might be more helpful than any confusing questions she might ask her brother.

Ozma smiled upward at the branches, hoping Kak might see her. She cast knowing glances to Maggie, Zim, Benny, Button Bright, and Jo, who looked upon the two ghosts. "Come, join us. I'm about to give them a tour of the Haunted Castle of Oz."

The End

NEED MORE ADVENTURE IN YOUR LIFE?

MYSTERY AND INTRIGUE IN
OOGABOO

Explore Oz!

The International Wizard of Oz Club

Membership brings rewards:

1. Three issues of the Club's premier journal *The Baum Bugle*, fully-illustrated with rare photographs and drawings, popular and scholarly articles on every aspect of the Oz phenomenon.
2. News in the world of Oz, including annual issues of *Oziana*, magazine featuring new Oz stories, and invites to upcoming conventions where you can meet fellow Oz fans, authors, and dealers.
3. Discounts on Club publications.

Join online at www.ozclub.org
or write:
The International Wizard of Oz Club, Inc.
P.O. Box 721129
Berkley, MI 48072-9998
USA

The Expanded Universe of Oz
Continuing the Original Canon Series

The Royal Explorers of Oz Quadrilogy

A new four-part series by Marcus Mebes, Jared Davis, and Jeff Rester explores long forgotten lands and secrets hidden about the Nonestic Continent. What ever happened to the pirates of Pirate Island from L. Frank Baum's *John Dough and the Cherub*? How about Prince Bobo from *Rinkitink in Oz*? What are the latest happenings in Ev, Ix, Mo, and even Ozamaland? Well, put on your best pirate gear and join us for a rollicking adventure around the entire continent... and beyond! Illustrated by Alejandro Garcia and John Troutman. *(Available in four volumes, hardcover and trade paperback, and in a forthcoming omnibus!)*

Sky Pyrates Over Oz

At long last! The finale to Sherwood Smith's Oz trilogy is here! Journey back to Oz with Dori and Emma, along with old favorites like Scraps and Polychrome, as they travel through the skies over Oz. There's a plot afoot with a dastardly villain who kidnapped Princess Dorothy in Smith's first book, *The Emerald Wand of Oz*. It'll take Glinda, Rikk the Nome, Dori, Emma, Scraps, and many more to contend with this threat... even a shaggy dog named "Dad!" Illustrated by Kim McFarland. *(Available in hardcover)*

Also Available
The Woggle-Bug Book, by L. Frank Baum
Zauberlinda, the Wise Witch, by Eva Katherine Gibson
Forever in Oz, by Melody Grandy
The Gardener's Boy of Oz, by Phyllis Ann Karr
Lurline and the White Ravens of Oz, by Marcus Mebes
Shipwrecked in Oz, by Marcus Mebes
The Bashful Baker of Oz, by Marcus Mebes
The Mysterious Caverns of Oz, by Marcus Mebes
...and much more!

The Expanded Universe of Oz
Continuing the Original Canon Series

The Law of Oz and Other Stories
The Magic Umbrella of Oz
Yookoohoos in Oz

Paul Dana takes readers through the lost history of Oz with intrepid explorers Button Bright and Ojo, who travel back to the time Queen Lurline first enchanted Oz! The boys discover the secrets behind the shape-shifting Yookoohoos, Phanfasms and the Wicked Witch of the East! Momentous changes and revelations will pit them against the very Law of Oz! Illustrated by Patricio Carbajal, Gabhor Utomo, Teresa Jenellen, Jaun Raza, and Vincent Myrand. *(Available in hardcover and trade paperback)*

Adolf Hitler in Oz

When Hitler fakes his own death, he winds up in Oogaboo in Oz, where he begins to gather an army for conquest. But to conquer Oz, he must first understand it, and in a land where there is no death, money or strife, that won't be easy. Includes thirty-five full and half-page illustrations by Patricio Carbajal, and the bonus essay, "The Utopia of Oz."
(Available in a hardcover deluxe edition with 11 color plates and exclusive stained-glass cover, and trade paperback edition)

Queen Ann in Oz

Picking up where L. Frank Baum left off, would-be conqueror Queen Ann of Oogaboo has vowed to find her lost parents, missing for decades. Accompanying her are the Shaggy Man, a young dragon named Moretomore, and a feisty group of volunteers eager for adventure! Includes the novella "Jodie in Oz" and "Another Adventure with Ann." Written by Oz alumni Eric Gjovaag and Karyl Carlson; illustrated by Bill Campbell & Irwin Terry. *(Available in deluxe hardcover with 15 color plates, and trade paperback edition)*

And Coming Soon!
The Immortal Longings of Oz
Skydroppers in Oz

www.ingramcontent.com/pod-product-compliance
Lightning Source LLC
Chambersburg PA
CBHW050513260626
47157CB00004B/1309